Sierra backed away. "I have to ask you not to do that again."

He nodded. "Agreed. It wouldn't be a good idea for you to get involved with me. I won't be around for long and, despite our little charade, I'm not very good boyfriend material."

Sierra hadn't expected him to agree with her so quickly. Disappointment filled her chest. Pushing back her shoulders, she lifted her chin. Why should she care? He'd only confirmed her desire to avoid anything sticky growing between them. Still...

He turned and walked toward the door.

Before he crossed the threshold, she asked, "Why?"

He stopped and half turned toward her. "Why what?"

"Why do you make bad boyfriend material?" She shouldn't be interested in his answer, but she was and she waited for his response.

He shook his head, a hint of a smile tilting his lips. "Trust me. I'm no good for you, or any other woman." With that, he walked out of the room and shut the door.

HOT VELOCITY

New York Times Bestselling Author
ELLE JAMES

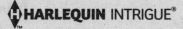

This book is dedicated to my grandmother who, at the age of 97, is still fighting to stay in this world. After a broken back, she powered her way through physical therapy to make it back home from rehab for Thanksgiving. She's a fighter and I hope to have as much gumption as she does when I'm 97!

Recycling programs for this product may not exist in your area.

ISBN-13: 978-1-335-72109-9

Hot Velocity

Copyright © 2017 by Mary Jernigan

Printed in U.S.A.

www.Harlequin.com

Elle James, a *New York Times* bestselling author, started writing when her sister challenged her to write a romance novel. She has managed a full-time job and raised three wonderful children, and she and her husband even tried ranching exotic birds (ostriches, emus and rheas). Ask her, and she'll tell you what it's like to go toe-to-toe with an angry 350-pound bird! Elle loves to hear from fans at ellejames@earthlink.net or ellejames.com.

Books by Elle James

Harlequin Intrigue

Ballistic Cowboys

Hot Combat
Hot Target
Hot Zone
Hot Velocity

SEAL of My Own

Navy SEAL Survival
Navy SEAL Captive
Navy SEAL to Die For
Navy SEAL Six Pack

Covert Cowboys, Inc.

Triggered
Taking Aim
Bodyguard Under Fire
Cowboy Resurrected
Navy SEAL Justice
Navy SEAL Newlywed
High Country Hideout
Clandestine Christmas

Visit the Author Profile page at Harlequin.com for more titles.

CAST OF CHARACTERS

Rex "T-Rex" Trainor—US marine on loan to the Department of Homeland Security for Task Force Safe Haven.

Sierra Daniels—Mother's Day Out Day Care worker who loves children and being independent.

"Hawkeye" Trace Walsh—US Army Airborne Ranger and expert sniper, on loan to the Department of Homeland Security for Task Force Safe Haven.

Kevin Garner—Agent with the Department of Homeland Security in charge of Task Force Safe Haven.

Jon "Ghost" Caspar—US Navy SEAL on loan to Department of Homeland Security for Task Force Safe Haven.

Max "Caveman" Decker—US Army Delta Force soldier on loan to the Department of Homeland Security for Task Force Safe Haven.

Clay Ellis—Sierra Daniels's ex-husband who hasn't accepted that they are divorced.

Grady Morris—Political candidate in the race for senator of Wyoming.

Bryson Rausch—Formerly the wealthiest resident of Grizzly Pass, who lost everything in the stock market.

Leo Fratiani—Land agent set on securing some land for an oil pipeline project.

Brenda Larson—Sierra Daniels's friend and coworker.

Chapter One

"Whatcha got?" Captain Rex "T-Rex" Trainor leaned toward the man sitting beside him in the helicopter, preparing to deploy into the small Afghan village on the edge of nowhere.

Gunnery Sergeant Lance Gallagher, Gunny to the unit, grinned, splitting his scarred, rugged face in two, and held up a small, shiny piece of paper with a black-and-white picture on it. "Number four is a boy!" he shouted over the roar of the rotors spinning overhead.

T-Rex nodded. "Congratulations!"

"Three girls and a boy." Gunny shook his head, his lips curling into a happy smile. "Poor kid will be outnumbered by women." He looked up, catching T-Rex's gaze, his smile fading. "That's why I'm giving up the good life of a career soldier to retire. I plan on being there to make sure Junior gets a shot at playing football, baseball and whatever the hell sport he wants."

T-Rex didn't blame the man. "Someone needs to be there to make sure he has that chance."

"Darn right." Gunny waved the thin piece of paper at T-Rex. "I want to teach him to throw his first ball, build a fort, take him hunting and, most of all…teach him how to treat a woman right." He winked.

What every boy needed—a father who cared enough to show him the ropes. T-Rex's dad had taught him everything he knew about horses, ranching and riding broncos in the rodeo. He'd taught him how to suck it up when he was thrown and to get back up on that horse, even when he was injured. Too many kids nowadays didn't have that parental influence, whether it be a mother or father, to push them to be all they could be and more.

"LZ coming up!" the pilot shouted. He lowered the craft onto the rocky ground and held steady while the team exited from both sides of the Black Hawk.

Although it was night, nothing stood in the way of the stars and the moon shining down on the rugged landscape.

They were deposited on the other side of a hill from their target village. In less than thirty minutes they climbed to the top of the ridge and half ran, half slid down the other side into the back wall of the hamlet.

This was supposed to be a routine sweep to ensure the small group of Taliban thugs they'd chased off hadn't returned. The intelligence guys had some concerns since the location was so close to the hills and caves the terrorists fled to when driven out of their strongholds.

T-Rex motioned for his team to spread out along the wall. When he gave the signal, they were to scale the wall and drop to the other side. When everyone was in position, he spoke softly into his mic. "Let's do this."

In two-man teams, they helped each other over the wall, landing softly on the other side. T-Rex led the way through the buildings, checking inside each one. The locals knew the drill, they'd been invaded so many times. They remained silent and gathered their sleeping children close.

What a life. These people never knew who was coming through the door next, or if the intruders would kill them all or let them live to see another day.

As T-Rex neared the other end of the village, doors stood open to huts that were empty of people and belongings.

The hairs on the back of his neck stood at attention. "Something's not right here," he said softly into his mic. He knelt in the shadow of a building and strained to see any movement in the street ahead or from the rooftops. Nothing moved. No shadows stirred or separated from the buildings, and no one loomed overhead from the tops of the homes.

In his gut, T-Rex knew they were walking into a trap. "Back out the way we came," he whispered.

"I've got your back," Gunny said.

"Get the others out of here. I smell a trap."

"Not going without you, sir," Gunny insisted.

"That's an order," T-Rex said, his tone firm, despite the whisper. "Move out." He glanced over his shoulder to the gunnery sergeant's position a building behind him, and on the opposite side of the road, the other members waited for the signal, hugging the shadows. At that moment, a shadow appeared on the roof directly over Gunny's head.

"Heads up! Tango over you, G," T-Rex warned, setting his sights on the man, waiting for the telltale shape of a weapon to appear. His finger on the trigger, T-Rex counted his breaths.

One...two...

The man yanked something in his hand.

"Not good!" T-Rex pulled the trigger, hitting the man in the chest. He collapsed forward, the object in his hand slipping from his grip, falling to the ground. "Grenade!" T-Rex shouted.

Gunny threw himself away from the small oval object rolling across the dirt. But not soon enough.

T-Rex lurched to his feet, too far away from his gunnery sergeant to be of any use. "No!"

The world erupted.

T-Rex was flung backward, landing hard on his back, the breath knocked from his lungs. Stunned, he lay for a second, staring up at the stars overhead, shining like so many diamonds in the sky until the dust and debris from the blast obliterated the night. Then he remembered how to breathe and sucked in a huge lungful of dust. The popping sound of gunfire came from above and all around.

T-Rex rolled toward the shadows of a building and bunched his legs beneath him. Bullets rained down around him, kicking up puffs of dirt near his feet.

Raising his weapon to his shoulder, T-Rex scanned the rooftops through the cloud of dust.

A man stood above him, aiming an AK47 in his direction.

His ears still ringing, T-Rex pinned the man in his sights and fired. One shot. The man fell to the ground, his weapon clattering on the rocky street.

T-Rex quickly scanned neighboring rooftops and the road ahead. Nothing moved there, but the world was pure chaos behind him.

He spun and ran toward the others, his heart hammering in his chest, his head still spinning from the detonation of the concussion grenade.

His men were pinned to the sides of the building, by a single fighter wielding a machine gun from his position near to where his comrade had been standing when T-Rex had taken him out.

T-Rex knelt, aimed, but his vision blurred. He blinked, gaining a clearer shot. His finger tightened on the trigger. He fired one round, and the fighter fell, dropping the machine gun to the street below.

Farther ahead, three of his men were exchanging gunfire with two fighters hiding out between the buildings. How the hell had they missed them?

Their training kicked in and they leap-frogged, providing each other cover as they worked their way to the fighters and knocked them out, one by one.

T-Rex hurried to where Gunny lay in the rubble of the building damaged by the grenade.

The man lay so still, T-Rex's gut knotted. He bent to feel for a pulse. At first, he could feel nothing. He held his breath and shifted his finger. That was when he felt the reassuring vibration of a heartbeat. Quickly scanning the man's arms and legs, he noted the tears in his clothing where shrapnel had penetrated. None of the wounds was bleeding profusely. If Gunny had sustained an arterial wound, T-Rex was prepared to apply a tourniquet. But he hadn't.

Chief Petty Officer Miles Kieslowski ran up to him. "Sir, we got incoming enemy reinforcements. We have to get out of here while we can." He stared down at the man covered in dust. "Damn." He glanced up into T-Rex's gaze. "Is he…"

"Alive. But I don't know the extent of his injuries."

"Let's get him out of here." Kieslowski started to lift Gunny. "Kenner is on the radio, calling in for pickup."

"No. I've got him," T-Rex said. "You cover me."

He handed his rifle to Kieslowski. With his hands free, he pulled Gunny to a sitting position and then draped the man's body over his shoulder. Straightening, he felt the strain on his back and legs. But nothing would stop him from bringing his man out. Never, in all of his skirmishes, had he left a man behind. He wouldn't start now.

With his burden, T-Rex hurried toward the designated extraction site. As he emerged from the village into the open, he spotted several trucks in the distance, stirring up dust as they barreled toward them. In the light from the moon, T-Rex could tell the men loaded in the backs of those trucks all carried weapons.

The thundering roar of helicopter rotors sounded nearby as the aircraft rose up over the hill behind the village and landed a couple of hundred yards from where T-Rex had stopped to catch his breath. The other marines from his team knelt behind him, firing at the village, as more enemy fighters came out of hiding.

T-Rex had one goal: to get his men to the waiting chopper and out of there before they were outnumbered. As he reached the helicopter, he gave over Gunny's care to the medic on board and turned toward his team.

Several of them ran toward him, while the others returned fire, backing up as they did. When they were out of range of rifle fire, they ran toward the aircraft and leaped in.

T-Rex stood beside the vehicle, helping his men board. When the last man was in, T-Rex climbed in, yelling, "Go! Go! Go!"

As he settled into his seat, he noted the trucks had stopped short of the village. Several men climbed out carrying long narrow tubes. "They've got RPGs!" he yelled.

The helicopter couldn't move fast enough for T-Rex. It lifted off the ground with its heavy load of souls on board and swung back toward the hill.

They had just made it to the ridge when an explosion went off so close, it made the chopper shudder.

Instinctively, T-Rex ducked.

They made it over the ridge and dropped out of the line of sight of the truck and the RPG-bearing fighters.

The rest of the trip back to their post seemed like they were moving in slow motion. The medics worked furiously over Gunny and the other men who'd sustained injuries.

"Is he going to make it?" T-Rex leaned over his gunnery sergeant, thoughts on that sonogram photo of the man's fourth child. The boy he'd always dreamed of having. For the first time in a long time, T-Rex closed his eyes and prayed.

Chapter Two

"Time to line up," Sierra Daniels called out to the toddlers on the playground outside the Grizzly Pass Community Center. Some of the little ones headed her way. Others ignored her completely and continued to play with their favorite outside toys or apparatus.

Sierra couldn't be angry with them. They were children with the attention spans of gnats, and so adorable she loved each one of them like she would her own. If she had any kids of her own. She sighed, pushing back against that empty feeling that always washed over her when she thought about how much she'd wanted to hold her own baby in her arms.

With a shrug, she called out again, forcing her voice to sound a little sterner. "Okay, ladies and gentlemen, it's time to line up for a game." Though they were all under six years old, they seemed to have a keen sense of who they could push around and who they couldn't. Sierra was 100 percent a push-over when it came to children.

Once all the boys and girls stood in front of her, Sierra instructed, "Let's play follow the leader. Hands on the shoulders of the one in front of you, like this." She placed the hands of one of the little girls on the shoulders of another. When each child had his or her hands on the one in front, Sierra led the little girl who was first in line around the play yard, weaving back and forth, creating a giggling, laughing snake of toddlers.

The community center had once been a US Army National Guard Armory. Eventually, the Montana National Guard moved its meeting location to a larger town and turned the building over to Grizzly Pass. It was now used as a community center for local events and the Mother's Day Out day care program. There were also several offices in the building rented out to local businesses.

Sierra had been ecstatic to land a job as a caregiver to the small children who were too young to go to public school. Jobs were hard to come by in the small community, and she'd needed one when she'd filed for divorce.

She and the other caregiver, Brenda Larson, worked together to corral the little ones and see that they were happy, fed and learned something while they were at the center.

Brenda was inside with the babies and infants. The two women traded off between the babies and the more mobile toddlers.

Sierra led the children around the yard one more time and had angled toward the door to the armory when a truck pulled up and the driver honked the horn.

Her fists clenched and she tried not to glare at the man stepping down from the vehicle. The children picked up on her moods more than she'd ever realized. If she was sad or angry, tiny Eloisa would pucker up and cry her little eyes out. It broke Sierra's heart to see the tiny girl with the bright red curls shed a single tear, much less a storm of them. She refused to give in to the temptation to yell and throw rocks at the man walking her way.

She pasted a fake smile on her face and waited until he was within twenty feet of her before she said in a patient but firm voice, similar to the one she used with her class, "Please, stop where you are." Her smile hurt her cheeks, but she refused to release it.

Clay Ellis crossed his arms over his chest. "Get your things. You're comin' home."

"I don't live with you, Clay," Sierra said, her voice singsong in an attempt to fool the children into thinking she was fine and that the angry man wasn't scaring her, and therefore they shouldn't be frightened either.

She glanced down at the thirteen children gathering closer around her knees.

Eloisa stared from Clay to Sierra, her bottom lip trembling.

Oh, no. Sierra wouldn't let Clay's bad temper impact the little ones. "Come on, everyone. It's time to go inside."

"Like hell it is." Clay stepped forward.

Eloisa screamed and flung her arms around Sierra's legs, burying her face in Sierra's slacks.

She laid her hand on the bright, soft curls and faced her ex-husband. "Clay, I'll have to ask you to leave. You're frightening the children."

He didn't leave. Instead, he walked up to her, grabbed her arm and pulled. "Quit playing around with these brats and get home. I've put up with enough of your nonsense."

Sierra dug in her heels, refusing to go anywhere with the jerk. She'd put up with enough of his verbal and physical abuse. "We aren't married anymore. You have no right to boss me around, now or ever. Let go of me."

He raised his free hand as if to strike her.

Sierra braced herself, but wouldn't flinch. There had been a time she'd cowered when he'd raised his hand to her. But not anymore. She'd learned the hard way that she had rights, and she didn't have to take abuse from any man.

The children clung to her, their eyes wide, scared. Eloisa sobbed loudly into the smooth linen of Sierra's tan slacks. Once Eloisa started, the other children sensed her distress and joined the squall.

"Shut up!" Clay yelled.

For a moment, all the children stopped crying and then, as if the spigot had been opened full blast, they all screamed and cried like a dozen caterwauling cats in a back-alley fight.

Clay yanked her out of the center of the noise and dragged her toward his truck.

Sierra dug her feet into the dirt and resisted with all of her might. "Let go of me. I'm not going with you."

"The hell you aren't," he said. "You belong to me."

"I belong to no man." She clawed at the meaty hand gripping her wrist like a vise. "I have a restraining order against you."

"No one's going to honor it. Everyone knows you're my wife."

"*Ex*-wife. What part of *divorce* don't you understand?" She couldn't let him get her into his truck. Sierra couldn't go back to this man. He was a bully, a cheater and a monster. "Let go of me, or I'll scream."

"Scream. Only those brats will hear you." He snorted. "You expect them to come to your rescue?"

"I don't need anyone to rescue me." She stopped leaning back against his hold on her and let him pull her close. When she was in range, she stomped hard on his instep and raised her knee hard against his crotch.

Clay bellowed and bent double, clutching the area she'd injured. But he didn't release his grip on her wrist.

Sierra's fingers were growing numb, and the kids behind her were hysterical. She had to do something to stop this madness. But what? Clay was bigger, stronger and meaner than she was. He'd demonstrated that over and over again. She had the scars to prove it.

"Please, Clay, you're scaring the children. Let me get them into the building. When I'm done, I'll go with you."

"Yeah, right." He grunted and straightened. "You expect me to believe you?"

"I will. Cross my heart." She held up her hand as if she were swearing in front of a jury, something she'd had to do in order to convince a judge she'd been abused and needed out.

"No way." He turned and dragged her closer to his truck.

"You can't leave them standing outside. They might get lost in the woods. They're just children."

"Like the kids you wouldn't give me? Why the hell should I care?"

"I wanted children. I tried," she said. "You can't blame our problems on these little ones."

"They aren't mine. I don't give a crap what happens to them."

When he set his mind on something, there was no stopping the man. He'd refused to listen to reason when they were married. What made Sierra think he would listen now?

Using another one of the techniques she'd learned in her recent self-defense class, she twisted her wrist, jerked her arm downward and broke free of Clay's hold. Free at last, she spun and ran. She hadn't gone two feet when a hand clamped on her hair and yanked her backward.

Sierra screamed and stumbled backward. The children screamed, as well. She could see them standing there, terrified and confused. It made her mad enough she could have spit nails, and all the more determined to free herself of the madman she'd once promised to love, honor and cherish.

"Well, it goes both ways. And you didn't live up to your part of the bargain," she muttered, twisted and turned, attempting to get away. But short of letting him rip chunks of her hair out of her head, she was caught.

Chapter Three

A persistent ringing grated on T-Rex's nerves. He didn't like to look away from the road when he was driving, so he waited until he pulled to a stop sign before glancing at his cell phone.

GALLAGER

The name on the screen made his heart tighten. The man had gotten out of that Afghan village alive, barely. He hadn't lost his life, but he'd lost so much more. "Hey, Gunny, how's that baby?"

"Great. I got to hold him today. With a little help."

T-Rex swallowed hard before saying, "That's great, man."

"Did I tell you that I'm getting some of the feeling back in my fingers?"

"No kidding?"

"No kidding." Gunny sounded more upbeat than T-Rex had heard him since he'd returned to the States. The hand squeezing his heart loosened a little. "Glad to hear it."

"I'll be throwing a football for slugger before long."

"Please tell me you didn't put 'Slugger' on his birth certificate."

"No. The wife wouldn't let me. Officially, he's Lance Gallagher. But I drew the line at Junior. Nothing shoots a man's ego down more than being called Junior."

"True."

"So, how's your TDY going?" Gunny asked. "About ready to head back to home station and ship out again?"

"Past ready."

"That boring?"

T-Rex had to think about that. "Not really boring, just not what I want to be doing."

"What? Kidnappings and big-game hunters not exciting enough?"

"How'd you know about that?" T-Rex asked.

Gunny snorted. "I read the news."

"I could do without some of the excitement. I want to get back to the front line."

"You know you won't find the guys who did this to us," Gunny said, his voice softening. "You could hunt every last member of the Taliban and still not know whether you got the guys who staged that trap."

"Maybe, but if I don't try, they get away with what they did to you."

"Oh, is this about me?" Gunny laughed. "The way

you blew up in front of the command psychologist, you'd think it was all about you."

T-Rex's hand squeezed the cell phone so hard, he was surprised it didn't crack. What he was feeling was in direct response to what had happened to Gunny. The man had taken the full brunt of the attack. He'd suffered spinal cord damage and might be a quadriplegic the rest of his life. The thought of the father of four spending his life in a wheelchair made T-Rex want to rage at the universe. "It's just not fair. I should have been the one injured. I didn't have a baby on the way."

"You didn't get to pick," Gunny said. "It's the way the cards fell. Or the grenade, in our case."

"Anyway, things might be settling down here. I feel like I'm spinning my wheels."

"Yeah, but I doubt the commander will want you back so soon. He was pretty hot when he sent you off."

"If he knew what a boondoggle it is, he wouldn't have sent me."

"Boondoggle?" Gunny snorted. "Sounds like another day in the life of a marine. You've got enemy hiding in the hills, you've been shot at and you've taken out some of the bad guys."

He had a point. Still, T-Rex would rather be back where his world had come apart. Then maybe he could put it back together. "I don't know which strings our team lead pulled to get a loan of highly skilled military men to work for the Department of Homeland Security." Luckily the team had been there, or there could have been a bunch of kids dead or trapped in a mine. "It's like the Wild West out here in Wyoming."

"Dude, Wyoming *is* the Wild West. Who lives there, anyway?"

"Exactly. Mostly a bunch of cowboys. There's not much more to do out here than ranching or work for the pipeline."

"What's wrong with that? You're in the most beautiful part of the country. Take in some fishing in your time off. If you get to know Wyoming, you might not hate it as much."

"I don't exactly hate it." He didn't. In fact, the area was beautiful. If he wasn't in the military, and maybe when he retired, he might consider living there. The rugged mountains were majestic and appeared serene. "I just want to get back to the real war."

"And some unhealthy fixation on retribution against the Taliban. Do you think you could do more good for the US in a foreign country than here at home?"

"There are other people who defend the home front."

"Clearly there aren't enough people with your skills in Wyoming." Gunny sighed. "Look, I'm not going to change your mind about the need for you to be where you are now. Let's change the subject."

T-Rex relaxed some of the tension from his shoulders. "Good."

"Good," Gunny agreed. "What have they got you doing now?"

T-Rex hadn't realized he'd slowed nearly to a stop on the main road until a honk reminded him he was in a truck and he should be driving to where he was supposed to go. He pressed his foot to the accelerator and the truck leaped forward. "I'm on my way to the County Records office to look up who owns property along an existing gas pipeline."

"Okay, now you're talking boring. I practically fell asleep as you talked about it." Gunny laughed. "Just kidding. Sounds like you're having to do a little sleuthing. That could be interesting."

T-Rex had to admit, after all they'd been through in the few weeks he'd been in Grizzly Pass, the need to resolve the open issues had crawled beneath his skin and stuck with him. "It's all part of figuring out who's behind the problems they've had lately in this little backwater town."

"I thought you caught the guy."

"We caught *some* of the guys we think were involved. But not the one who had enough money to purchase a couple crates full of AR-15 rifles for distribution. Nor have we found those missing rifles."

"You think you have something bigger going on? Wow. You are in up to your eyeballs."

"Maybe. Or maybe we're marking time. If someone is truly out there planning a takeover of a government facility, they might be lying low until the Department of Homeland Security releases us military augmentees. Then they'll do their damage."

T-Rex turned onto the street that would lead him to the Grizzly Pass Community Center and the County Records office. As he pulled into the parking lot, he noted a truck, with a mashed front fender, parked at an odd angle, taking up more than its share of the available parking spaces. But that wasn't all. A man was dragging a woman by the hair toward the truck. By the expression on her face, she wasn't at all happy about it.

"Gunny, I gotta go." Without waiting to hear his friend's response, he dropped the cell phone into the cup holder, slammed the shift into Park and slid out of the truck, his hands balling into fists. Nothing made him madder than witnessing a man abusing a woman.

SIERRA STRAINED HER NECK, trying to get Clay to release his hold on her hair. "Let go of me. I have a job to do. I have children to take care of."

"You have a husband to take care of, and you're not doing it here."

"We. Aren't. Married," she said through gritted teeth. The pain of having her hair pulled so hard brought tears to her eyes.

A loud crack sounded behind Sierra.

Clay grunted and dropped to the ground, taking her with him.

Sierra fell to her backside. Clay's hand loosened its hold on her hair. She rolled to the side, bunched her legs and shot to her feet, putting several feet between her and Clay before she looked back and came to a complete stop.

Clay lay on the ground, his hand clamped over his cheek.

A big man with massive shoulders and an iron jaw loomed over Clay.

"Who the hell do you think you are?" Clay demanded.

The big guy growled. Literally growled. "Your worst nightmare if you lay another finger on that woman."

Sierra watched in wonder. The children gathered around her legs, clinging to her, shaking in their fright.

"I'll do whatever the hell I want," Clay said. "That woman's my wife."

"Ex-wife," Sierra reminded him.

"I don't care if she's your great-aunt Sue." The man poked a finger at Clay. "If you ever lay another hand on her, you'll have to reckon with me. Do. You. Understand?"

"I don't have to take this." Clay rolled to his feet and came up swinging.

The big guy ducked and, in one smooth uppercut, popped Clay in the chin, knocking him to the ground again. This time, Clay lay for a moment, blinking. "I'll kill you for that."

"Big talk for a man who can only seem to push *women* around."

Clay rubbed his bruised chin. "You gonna let me get up?"

"You gonna apologize to the lady?" He tipped his head toward Sierra.

Her ex-husband's lip curled into a snarl. "Ain't got nothin' to apologize for. *She's* the one who walked out on *me*."

The big guy shot a glance at Sierra. "Seems to me she had reason."

"That's a load of bull." Clay started to rise.

Big Guy pushed his foot into Clay's chest. "Not until you apologize."

Clay's cheeks burned a ruddy red and a muscle ticked in his jaw.

Sierra held her breath. She'd never seen Clay apologize for anything.

"I'm sorry," Clay said, his voice tight and angry, not apologetic in the least.

"Say it like you mean it," Big Guy warned, his fist clenching.

The color deepened in Clay's cheeks and his lips formed a thin line. "Fine. I'm sorry," he said, his tone measured, softer this time, but just as tight, the anger simmering between the surface.

Big Guy stepped back.

Clay rolled over, pushed to his hands and knees and staggered to an upright position, glaring at the man. "Who the hell are you anyway? And don't give me that crap about being my worst nightmare. What makes you think you can get in between me and my wife?"

"Ex-wife," Sierra repeated. "The divorce has been final for months. I have the signed copy to prove it."

"Not in my mind." Clay turned toward Sierra, his gaze boring into hers, his hands tightening into fists. "I never would have signed that paper if the judge hadn't threatened to throw me in jail."

Sierra planted her fists on her hips. "Yeah, well, it's done, legal and final. I'm not going back to you. I have a life now. And it doesn't include you."

Clay shot a look at Big Guy. "But it includes him? What? Is he your new boyfriend?"

Sierra lifted her chin. "If he was, it's none of your business."

Clay's eyes narrowed and he studied Big Guy. "So, you ditched me to hop in bed with him?"

"If she did, it has nothing to do with you." Big Guy crossed his arms over his massive chest and stood with his feet braced slightly apart, like a conquering warrior. "What she does is her own business."

Sierra's heart fluttered. By all appearances, Big Guy was a man's man. He didn't need to push a woman around to make himself feel big. He was larger than life and, at that moment, a hero in her eyes.

"Yeah, well, you can't be everywhere she is." Clay faced her. "I'll see you when your boyfriend isn't around."

Sierra's cheeks heated at Clay's reference to the stranger being her boyfriend. She figured now wasn't the time to correct him. Perhaps if Clay thought the guy who'd kicked his butt was her boyfriend, he'd be less likely to target her. "Just leave me alone, Clay."

"You belong to me," her ex said. "No hulking ape takes what's mine."

"Okay, buddy." Big Guy gripped Clay's arm and marched him toward his truck. "I can take a man swinging at me and I can take some verbal abuse, but when you start calling me a hulking ape, I draw the line." He opened the door and shoved Clay into the driver's seat. "Leave my girlfriend alone, or you'll be reckoning with me." Then he slammed the door and stepped clear of the truck.

Sierra held her breath, fully expecting Clay to push the truck into gear and run Big Guy over.

Clay lowered his window and yelled, "It ain't over."

"Oh, yes, it is." Brenda Larson stepped out of the building with a phone in her hands. "The sheriff is on his way."

Clay slammed his truck into Reverse and backed up so fast, his tires spit up gravel. He swung around and left the parking lot and Sierra in stunned silence.

Brenda waved. "Gotta get back to my babies."

"Go. I'll get the kids inside." Sierra waved toward her friend. Brenda ducked back inside, leaving Sierra with Big Guy and the thirteen crying children, clutching her legs.

"Are you all right?" her hero asked, turning his full attention to her. He had reddish-brown hair, cut high and tight like a military man, and his eyes could have been brown or green depending on the way he turned his head toward the sunshine.

Sierra gulped and tried to remember his question. "Uh, yes. I'm okay." She rubbed her arm absently.

"Did he hurt you? You know, you can file a report." The man closed the distance between them and took her hand, his face darkening. "He did hurt you."

Sierra stared down at the bruises forming on her arm. She pulled against his grip. "I'm fine. Right now, I need to get these children calm and inside."

Eloisa sobbed against her leg, clutching Sierra so tightly, she couldn't move without knocking the little girl over.

Several of the children who couldn't get close enough to Sierra turned to Big Guy and wrapped their arms around his legs, crying.

Sierra laughed and gulped back a ready sob. "I'm sorry. But it seems we are trapped by a handful of toddlers." She held out her hand, forcing herself to sound normal and upbeat, putting a game face on for the children. "I'm Sierra Daniels. And you are?"

"Apparently, I'm your boyfriend." His lips curled into a sexy smile that nearly bowled her over. "Rex Trainor. My friends call me T-Rex."

Sierra raised her brows. "As in the dinosaur?"

He nodded. "That's right." He engulfed her hand with his big one.

Warmth flowed all the way up her arm and into her chest. "Thank you for coming to my rescue… T-Rex." She glanced down at the toddlers. "Okay, gang, the show's over and everybody's okay. Let's go play in the gym."

"I want my mommy," Eloisa wailed. Sierra lifted her small body and settled the redhead on her hip.

Several other children joined in the chorus.

"Who wants a ride into the gym?" T-Rex reached down and lifted a little boy named Nathan and settled him on his shoulders.

At first the little boy's lip trembled, and then he gripped T-Rex's hair, grinned and giggled.

"Who else?" T-Rex asked. With Nathan clinging to his hair, Sierra's hero scooped up a little girl and a boy in his arms. "Follow me!" he called out in the best impression of a drill sergeant's tone Sierra had heard in a long time.

Without hesitation, the rest of the toddlers lined up behind T-Rex and marched with him into the community center.

Sierra hugged Eloisa against her chest and followed. This must have been what it felt like to follow the Pied Piper. She didn't know this man, but she trusted him with her life and those of the toddlers in her care.

And if he had hazel eyes that she could fall into and dark, reddish-brown hair she'd like to run her fingers through, that shouldn't matter in the least. He'd come to her rescue. That made him a hero in her eyes and the eyes of the children.

Her heart beat faster and butterflies fluttered their wings inside her belly. Her day was looking up. And all because of a stranger who'd arrived in time to save the day. Talk about heroes.

Chapter Four

T-Rex entered through a side door that led into an open gymnasium with brick walls and basketball goals on either end.

A woman stood in one of the open doorways off the side of the gym, a baby in her arms. "Oh!" She blinked several times. "I was expecting Sierra. Who are you?"

His lips twisted into an ironic grin. "Apparently, I'm Sierra's boyfriend."

"He's kidding." The woman he'd rescued from her ex-husband entered behind him, carrying a tiny red-haired girl. Sierra's cheeks were rosy and her blue eyes bright. "Clay assumed he was my boyfriend." She shrugged. "I didn't disavow him of that assumption."

"Like I said. I'm her new boyfriend."

Sierra's friend stared at him, her eyes narrowing. "Wait. You're one of the new guys in town working with Kevin Garner, aren't you?"

T-Rex nodded and set down the children in his arms and then swung the little boy off his shoulders to his screaming delight.

As soon as he set him on the ground, the boy reached up. "Do it again! Do it again! Please?"

T-Rex lifted the boy high into the air and swung him back to the ground.

The other toddlers all raised their hands, shouting, "My turn!" at the top of their lungs.

"Okay, children," Sierra called out over the commotion. "Mr. Trainor isn't here to entertain all of you. Let him go about his business. Go on and play." She set the red-haired girl on her feet and shooed her and the others toward the tumbling mats scattered across a corner of the gym. Once the children had moved away, Sierra held out her hand. "Thank you so much for coming to my rescue."

He gripped her small hand in his, and a shock of electricity raced up his arm. His gaze connected with hers. Had she felt it? Her eyes widened for a second, but other than that little bit of motion, she didn't indicate recognition.

Her lips curled upward in a smile. "Are you done with my hand?"

T-Rex immediately released her and jammed his hand into his pocket. "My pleasure."

"Seriously, Sierra," the woman with the baby on her hip said. "You haven't met the men from the team of military guys who helped save us when the bus was hijacked?"

She shook her head. "Actually, I haven't. You remember. When that happened, I was out with the flu."

"You're the one they called T-Rex, right?" The woman walked forward. "You might not remember me, but I'm Brenda Larson. We met in front of the Lucky Lou Mine a few days ago, after the showdown with the Vanders boys."

T-Rex shook her hand. "I'm sorry. I don't remember."

"I can understand. There was a lot going on." Brenda's lips thinned and she glanced at Sierra. "Be glad you were sick that day. I still have nightmares."

Sierra shuddered. "I'm so sorry for Mrs. Green. Her husband was such a nice man."

"Mr. Green, the bus driver?" T-Rex asked.

Sierra and Brenda nodded.

"It was a shame. He didn't do anything to deserve being shot," T-Rex said.

"Well, don't let us keep you, Mr. Trainor," Sierra said. "Thanks again." She stepped back, out of his way.

A baby's cry had Brenda moving toward the door she'd come out of. "That's my cue. Nice to see you again, T-Rex."

T-Rex shook his head and glanced around. "I

understand the County Records office is somewhere in this building."

Sierra nodded. "You have to go back out to the front of the armory to get to their offices."

"This was an armory?"

"It used to house a small unit of the Montana Army National Guard. When they moved out, they donated the building to the town. Now it's the Grizzly Pass Community Center."

He swept the gym with another assessing glance. Now that she'd mentioned it, he could imagine a military unit holding formations in the gym when the weather outside was too cold, wet or snowy. A twinge of regret filled his belly. While he was pretty much playing the civilian Stateside, members of his unit were putting their lives on the line in some god-forsaken country on the other side of the world. His fists clenched. "Nice that the building could be useful." As much as he'd like to talk to the pretty woman with the long, wavy blond hair, he had work to do. The sooner they figured out who was at the bottom of all the troubles in Grizzly Pass, the sooner he could be back with his unit.

Besides, it would do him no good to get close to a female. His career was with the US Marine Corps. And he'd seen the devastation a career in the military could wreak on a family. He couldn't do that to a woman, any more than he could do what Sierra's ex-husband had done to her. No, he was single for a reason. Career military men had no business dragging families along with them.

"I'll be going. If your ex gives you any more trouble, you can call me. I'll be happy to step in as the protective boyfriend for as long as I'm here." As long as that was as far as it went. He didn't say it, but he thought it, specifically to remind him he wasn't in Grizzly Pass to start anything. He was there to finish it.

He spun and walked out of the building and around to the front, where an entrance led into a hallway with what had once been the offices of the officers and enlisted men who'd run the unit. Now the doors were marked with the names of businesses. He found the one marked County Records and entered.

With the help of the clerk, he found the surveys and plats of the properties bordering the oil pipeline running through the hills on the south side of Yellowstone National Park.

He snapped photos with his cell phone, and on a notepad he jotted down the names of the people or corporations who owned the land. When he was finished, he tucked his notepad into his pocket. "Thank you," he called out as he left the office. He'd been there for over an hour. He knew he should go straight to his truck and leave, but he couldn't without first checking on Sierra. Back around the side of the armory, he found the entrance to the gym and day care.

Sierra stood with the little red-haired girl and a woman with equally red hair who had to be the child's mother.

"She took a nap after the commotion, but she might continue to be distressed," Sierra was saying. "I'm so sorry it happened in front of the children."

The mother held her daughter close in her arms. "I'm just glad you're okay. Don't you worry about us. Take care of yourself." The woman turned and stopped, her eyes wide. "Oh. I didn't hear you come in." Her eyes narrowed and she shot a glance back at Sierra. "Do you know him? I can stay if you need me to."

Sierra smiled. "I know him. He's the one who chased Clay away. The kids love him."

As if on cue, the little red-haired toddler reached her arms up to T-Rex. "My turn."

Her mother frowned.

"It's okay." Sierra nodded. "T-Rex had them all wanting a turn."

Eloisa leaned farther out.

T-Rex grabbed her before she fell from her mother's arms. "Do you mind?"

"I guess not." Eloisa's mother gave him a confused smile. "She doesn't usually go to strangers."

T-Rex swung her up into the air and back to the ground, then up again.

Eloisa giggled and laughed. When he handed her back to her mother, she clapped her hands and held them out. "Again."

"Sorry, sweetie." Her mother straightened the child on her hip and hiked her diaper bag up onto her shoulder. "We have to get home and cook supper." She smiled, waved and exited, leaving Sierra alone in the gym with T-Rex.

"Are all of the others gone?" he asked.

"Everyone but me." She retrieved her purse from a chair and slipped it over her shoulder. "I get to lock up tonight."

"I'll wait."

"You don't have to."

"I know." He waved a hand, indicating she should lead the way.

"Really. I can do this on my own."

He touched her arm. "Look, you're giving chivalry a bad name. After what happened today, I would feel better knowing you made it home safely."

Her baby blue eyes sparkled, and her cheeks turned a pretty shade of pink. She pushed her long blond hair back over her shoulders. "Okay, then." She led the way to the door.

T-Rex's gut twisted and his groin tightened as

she sailed past him, her slim hips swaying ever so slightly in her tan slacks.

He liked what he saw. Normally he would go after her and ask her out on a date. But his usual MO was to date and ditch. Based on what he'd witnessed of how her ex-husband had treated her, he couldn't do that to Sierra. She needed a man who treated her like a princess, with all the love and caring she deserved. This woman was strictly off-limits.

She led him out of the building, closed the door and locked it behind them.

"So, you're here with the others who've been loaned to the Department of Homeland Security?" she asked as they walked side by side to their vehicles.

"I am." He paused beside her older-model sedan and waited for her to pop the locks. When she had, he opened the door for her.

She glanced up at him. "Thank you for all you did today."

"You're welcome." She stood so close he could smell the subtle scent of her perfume. If he leaned forward just a little, he could capture her mouth with his. His pulse quickened and his gaze slipped from her shining blue eyes to those soft, full kissable lips.

"I... I'd better go. It's getting dark." She slipped into the car, closed the door and started the engine.

T-Rex stepped back, telling himself he was a fool

to even think about kissing the woman. She was on the rebound from a bad marriage. He'd be doing her a favor to stay out of her life.

Sierra lowered the window. "If ever I can do anything for you, don't hesitate to ask. I owe you bigtime."

He nodded, tempted to collect on her debt by requesting a kiss. Instead, he shook his head. "No repayment required. Just being a good citizen. I'll follow you to make sure you get home okay."

"This is a small town. It's not necessary." She smiled and backed out of the parking lot.

T-Rex waited until she disappeared down the winding drive heading away from the community center. Then he climbed into his truck and drove to his temporary quarters at a bed-and-breakfast off Main Street.

As he pulled into the parking lot, he noticed that one of the other vehicles parked at the very end looked familiar. He parked and got out. Could it be? He entered the big, rambling colonial home the owner had converted into a six-room bed-and-breakfast. Standing in the large living area was Sierra, talking to the owner, Mrs. McCall, two suitcases on the floor beside her.

She looked up as he entered, and her brow furrowed. "You didn't have to follow me."

"Mr. Trainor, I'm glad I caught you. I hope you

don't mind, but I had the handyman here today. He worked on the balcony door to keep it from sticking."

"Thank you, Mrs. McCall," he said, his gaze on Sierra, not the owner of the bed-and-breakfast.

"Oh, have you met Miss Daniels?" Mrs. McCall asked.

T-Rex nodded. "I have had the pleasure."

"She'll be staying with us while her apartment is being renovated."

He nodded. "That's nice. You'll love Mrs. McCall. She makes the best scones this side of the pond."

Mrs. McCall blushed. "Oh, you're too kind. Thank you."

"No need to tell me about her scones." Sierra smiled and patted Mrs. McCall's arm. "I've been eating Mrs. McCall's scones since I was a little girl visiting her with my mother. And you're right. They're wonderful."

"Thank you, sweetie." Mrs. McCall smiled and pushed back her shoulders. "Now, if you'll excuse me, my program is coming on television and I don't want to miss it." She winked. "An old woman needs something to look forward to." She scurried away, entering a door marked Private.

"Let me help you." T-Rex grabbed the handles of the suitcases.

"I can do that," Sierra said, reaching for the cases.

"I know you can. But we've already had this discussion about chivalry. It isn't dead. At least not where I'm concerned. My mother taught me better." He headed for the stairs. "What room?"

She gave him the number, and his brows rose. It was the room next to his. He wanted to groan, but he didn't say anything. She'd find out soon enough.

For a man who didn't want to start something with the pretty day care employee, the odds were stacking against him.

"I didn't know you were staying here," she said as she followed him up the stairs.

"In a town as small as Grizzly Pass, the lack of hotels forced us to scatter out among the few privately owned establishments." He stopped in front of the door to her room and stepped back to allow her to use her key in the lock.

She entered and held the door for him to carry her luggage through.

T-Rex set the two cases on the wooden floor and turned. "Welcome to the McCall house."

Sierra giggled. "You don't look like a bellboy, but I appreciate the help." She reached her hand into her purse and dug around. "What do you require in the way of a tip?"

He laid his hand on her arm. "No money. Just this." Before he could stop to question his motives, he lifted her chin with the tip of his finger and claimed that kiss he'd been thinking about since she'd left him

at the community center. One quick, toe-curling kiss.
That was all he wanted and he'd be out of her way.

But it didn't happen like he planned. As soon as
his lips touched hers, fire exploded in his belly and
his blood ran like heated mercury through his veins,
angling downward to his groin.

He raised his other hand, cupped the back of her
head and deepened the connection.

She laid her hands on his chest, but she didn't
push him away.

And he was glad she didn't. Because, now that he
was kissing her, he didn't want it to end.

SIERRA HAD BEEN shocked and tinglingly aware of the
man when he'd stepped through the front door of the
bed-and-breakfast. She'd completely forgotten what
she'd been saying to Mrs. McCall. All she'd been
able to do was stand there and stare at the broad-
shouldered hero with the reddish-brown hair and
hazel eyes, and just barely been able to stop herself from drooling. He was the kind of man every
girl dreamed of. Tall, dark, handsome and willing
to fight for her honor.

Now he stood in her room, kissing her. Her knees
trembled and she curled her fingers into his shirt,
pulling him closer. She raised up on her toes, deep-
ening the kiss of all kisses. Clay had never kissed
her like this. Like she was special and the only per-

son in the world. She pressed her body into T-Rex, loving the hardness of his muscles against her soft curves. He was a man a woman could lean on in tough times. He didn't need to have his ego stroked to make him feel more of a man.

His tongue darted out, tracing the line of her lips. She couldn't resist him, opening her mouth to allow him in. Part of her felt a little guilty. She had to remind herself she was single now. She could kiss anyone she liked. And she liked kissing this one.

He caressed her tongue with his, gliding in and out, taking her along on a rising wave of passion. The only thing that could have been better about that kiss was if they were both naked. Skin to skin.

Heat built low in her belly. An intense ache made her sex clench and her body long for more. She felt more alive than she had in years, and it was all due to this stranger, who asked for a kiss for his tip.

All too soon, T-Rex lifted his head.

Sierra dropped back onto her heels and glanced down at where her hands crumpled his shirt. She licked her swollen lips, tasting him on them. "Well, that was quite the tip," she managed to say, appalled at how squeaky her voice sounded.

"I'd apologize," he said, his tone low and husky. "But I can't. That was incredible."

She nodded and dared to look up into his eyes. Then reality set in. Having divorced only six months before, she wasn't sure she was ready to get right back into a relationship. If anything, her seven years of marriage to Clay had convinced her that she wasn't very good at long-term commitment, or was she just terrible at choosing the right man for her? Either way, it was too soon.

Sierra backed away. "I have to ask you not to do that again."

He nodded. "Agreed. It wouldn't be a good idea for you to get involved with me. I won't be around for long, and, despite our little charade, I'm not very good boyfriend material."

Sierra hadn't expected him to agree with her so quickly. Disappointment filled her chest. Pushing back her shoulders, she lifted her chin. Why should she care? He'd only confirmed her desire to avoid anything sticky growing between them. Still…

He turned and walked toward the door.

Before he crossed the threshold, she asked, "Why?"

He stopped and half turned toward her. "Why what?"

"Why do you make bad boyfriend material?" She shouldn't be interested in his answer, but she was and she waited for his response.

He shook his head, a hint of a smile tilting his lips. "Trust me. I'm no good for you, or any other woman." With that, he walked out of the room and shut the door.

All of the starch leached out of Sierra's shoulders and she sagged, raising her fingers to her mouth. Holy hell, the man could kiss. Her brows dipped and her eyes narrowed. And what kind of nonanswer was that? *I'm no good for you, or any other woman.*

Her curiosity aroused and left unsatisfied, she yanked one of the suitcases up onto the bed and began the task of unpacking. Within minutes, she had both cases emptied and her meager belongings stored in the dresser and closet. Six months ago, she'd left most of what she owned with Clay, taking only what she could carry in the cases. The apartment she'd been living in had come fully furnished. Unfortunately, the roof had sprung a leak in the last rain. Not only had they had to repair the roof, they'd had to rip out the drywall and flooring due to water damage and mold. She wouldn't be allowed back into the apartment until they'd completed all of the repairs and mold remediation. Thus, the move to the bed-and-breakfast.

The night was still young, the sun having barely dipped below the hilltops. She could lie there and reminisce or go find something to eat.

Grabbing her coat and purse, she headed for the door, slung it open and nearly crashed into T-Rex. "Oh, sorry."

He steadied her with his big hands and then dropped them to his sides. "Are you all right?"

"I'm fine." She stepped back and willed her heart to slow.

"I was coming to see you."

"You were?" Her pulse leaped again.

T-Rex dug in his pocket and pulled out a device that fit in the palm of his hand. "I want you to have this." He reached for her hand and placed it on her palm.

"What is it?" she stared down at the gadget, her heart banging against her ribs at the touch of his hand beneath hers.

"A stun gun."

Okay, so it wasn't a diamond bracelet, but seriously, what man gave a woman a stun gun as a gift? "How does it work?"

He turned it over and pointed to the button on the side. "You switch it on here. When someone gets close enough to you, you push this button and stick it to him."

"And then what?"

"He will lose muscle control and balance and become disoriented. It will disable him for up to thirty minutes."

"Wow." She held it out. "Sounds dangerous."

"The effects aren't permanent. It gives you a chance to get away. Carry it in your hand when you're alone, like when you're locking up at the day care and walking out to your car. If your ex ever pulls a stunt like he did today you can be ready to take him down long enough to get away. One jolt from this baby and he'll think twice about harassing you."

She stared at the device and then glanced up at him. "That's about the nicest gift anyone has ever given me."

He laughed out loud. "Better than roses?"

"Much." She slid it into her purse, careful not to switch it on in the process. "I'm not sure I have the nerve to use it, but it will make me feel better knowing I have it in case I need it."

"Were you heading out?" he asked.

"I was just going to find something to eat. Normally, I fix a salad and eat at home." She grimaced. "But that won't be an option while I live in the bed-and-breakfast. I miss my apartment already."

"I was about to go to the Blue Moose Tavern. Care to join me?"

She smiled and shook her head. "So much for avoiding each other. I think it will be nearly impossible in such a small house."

"No need to. I promise—" he held up his hand as if swearing in court "—not to overstep your boundaries without your permission."

"In that case, I would love the company. I hate

eating alone." She led the way down the stairs and out of the building.

Once outside, he glanced around as if looking for something or someone. "I don't see your ex anywhere, but we should probably keep up appearances." T-Rex held out his hand. "Girlfriend?"

She hesitated, staring at his big, open hand. Knowing it would only be for appearances, it shouldn't be a big deal. But as soon as she placed her hand in his, the electricity of his touch zipped through her body, pooling low in her groin. Yeah, being this close to T-Rex could only lead to trouble.

At that moment, she didn't care.

Together, they walked the three blocks to the Blue Moose Tavern and asked the waitress for a table.

Once seated across from T-Rex, her hand in her own lap and no longer touching the man, Sierra's thoughts settled from the scramble they'd been since she'd kissed him. He was just a man. The first man she'd kissed since her divorce. Surely there would be more, and she wouldn't make such a complete fool of herself over the next.

The waitress brought them their drinks—a glass of red wine for Sierra and a draft beer for T-Rex.

Sierra lifted her glass. "To new friends."

He touched his mug to her glass. "To new friends."

They sipped and stared over the tops of their respective drinks.

Sierra had to focus on staring into his eyes and not letting her gaze fall to his sensuous mouth. For a long moment, she struggled to come up with something to say that wasn't *kiss me*. Finally, she knocked back the rest of her wine and set her glass on the table. "Tell me about yourself."

Chapter Five

T-Rex felt his muscles tighten. He'd never been this uncomfortable sitting across a table from a beautiful woman. When she stared at him and demanded he tell her about himself, his pulse kicked up a notch. He swallowed the last of his beer and set down his mug. What did she really want to know?

Did she want to hear that he'd watched his best gunnery sergeant nearly get blown apart? That he wished he could have taken Gunny's place in that explosion? That he loved women but avoided relationships because of the profession he'd chosen to dedicate his life to? He didn't want to talk about himself, so he stalled. "Like what?"

"Not going to make this easy, are you?" Sierra nodded, squared her shoulders and launched. "You can start by telling me which branch of the service you're in."

"Marine Corps." That wasn't so hard. He relaxed a little.

"How long?" she demanded.

"Ten years."

"That's quite a commitment." She drew in a breath and let it out. "Have you been deployed to a war zone?"

Tension shot up again. He nodded, his glance dropping to his empty mug. "Four times."

Sierra's brows drew together, and she reached across the table, laying her hand on his arm. "Thank you for your service."

The heat of her touch sent his blood burning through his veins. He didn't feel like he had done anything to be thanked for. While he was walking around on two perfectly good legs, Gunny couldn't even hold his newborn son in his arms, or hug his girls.

T-Rex shook off her touch and moved his hands to his lap. "My turn."

She nodded. "Shoot."

"How long were you married to your charming husband?"

"Seven years."

"Was he as abusive the entire time you two were married?"

Sierra glanced to the far corner of the room, her brows wrinkled. "He's always been demanding. I thought he'd mellow as we grew older together, but he didn't. Then he lost his job as a truck driver due to an accident a couple years ago. He was home all the time and I went to work. That's when he got mean."

"Children?"

She shook her head, her shoulders sinking a degree. "No. No children."

"By choice, or luck of the draw?"

"It just didn't happen. If I could, I'd have a dozen children."

"Do you come from a big family?"

She shook her head. "No. My parents died when I was six. I was raised in the foster care system."

"I'm sorry."

"Don't be." She smiled. "My foster parents were very good to me."

"Were?"

She sighed. "They passed away within months of each other five years ago. I miss them."

"No siblings?" he asked.

She shook her head. "You?"

T-Rex nodded. "I have a sister in Texas. She's married with three little boys."

Sierra looked at him with a smile. "They must love their Uncle T-Rex."

"I doubt it." He shrugged. "I don't see them often enough." Hell, he hadn't seen them since they were all in diapers. He made a mental note to visit his sister.

"Parents?"

"Retired and traveling around the country in a motor home." He shook his head. "They sold the home and ranch we grew up on and bought a motor coach. They never spend more than four months in any one place. Their goal is to explore every national park in the United States before they die. And a few dozen state parks."

Sierra leaned her elbows on the table and rested her chin in her palm. "Wow, sounds like a wonderful way to spend your retirement." A long strand of her blond hair fell forward over her cheek.

Without thinking, T-Rex reached across the table and tucked it behind her ear. He brushed his knuckles across her cheek, that same electric current sending shock waves through his system. He snatched back his hand. "Why do you stay here?"

She shrugged. "I love this town and most of the people in it. Minus one ex-husband. It's a great place to live and raise a family."

"But you aren't married and, from what you've just told me, you don't have family here."

She shrugged. "I'd love to travel, but I never considered doing it alone." Her lips twisted. "I'd want to share my adventures with someone else. I couldn't see myself standing at the edge of the Grand Canyon and having no one to share my appreciation for what I'd be seeing." Sierra laughed. "Sounds dumb, but that's how I feel. Besides, I was married from the time I left college until just a few months ago. We didn't have the money to travel. We barely had enough to pay the rent. So, there you have it. That's my pathetic life in a nutshell. The best part about it is working with the children. I love those kids."

"And they all love you."

"The little traitors were quick to switch their loyalties when you came through the door." She winked at him. "Why don't you have children?" Her eyes widened suddenly. "Wow, I don't even know if you're married." She pressed her hand to her lips.

He shook his head. "I'm not, and I don't have any children." Leaning toward her, he said in a low voice for only her ears, "Besides, I wouldn't have kissed you if I had a wife. Call me old-fashioned, but I believe you only kiss the one you're committed to."

Sierra sank back against her seat. "Whew. You never know. I've been out of the dating scene for a long time. Heck, I don't think I've ever been in it. I married my high school sweetheart two years into college."

"What did you major in?" he asked.

"I would have majored in elementary education, but I didn't get to finish." She rubbed the third finger on her left hand.

"Why?"

"Clay thought college was a waste of time. He dropped out and got a job as a truck driver and we got married. When it came time for fall semester to start, he wouldn't let me go back. He said it cost too much, and what did I need a college education for anyway? He made enough money driving a truck to support us."

"And he lost his license."

She nodded. "Over a year ago."

"Seven years and no children. That from a woman who loves kids." He raised his brows.

"I wanted them." She shrugged and looked away. "They never seemed to happen. Can we talk about something else?"

"Sorry. I didn't mean to pry."

"It's okay. It was a sore subject in our marriage, and it still hurts."

"Then let's talk about what to order." He popped open a menu and perused the items he had yet to try. Soon, the waitress delivered a bison burger for him and a Southwestern chicken salad for Sierra. They spent the rest of the meal talking about the upcoming football season and who they thought would play in the bowl games.

When he'd finished the burger and fries, he ordered another beer and sat back. "I'm surprised you know your college football teams."

She sipped from her wineglass and raised her brows. "Why? Because I'm a girl?"

"No," he hedged. "Because you're a woman. I thought most women disliked sports."

"That's a sexist remark."

"Guilty."

"My foster mother and father were huge football fans. We spent many weekends watching the games and yelling until our throats were raw." She smiled, her face softening. "I miss that."

"Was your ex a fan?"

She shook her head. "He liked hockey. Don't get me wrong. I love watching a good hockey game, too. But I missed watching football."

"He wouldn't let you watch football?"

"No."

"Jerk," T-Rex muttered just loud enough for her to hear.

Sierra laughed. "My thoughts exactly." For a long moment, her smile lingered. Then it disappeared altogether.

T-Rex found himself wanting to make her smile again.

"Speak of the devil." Sierra nodded toward the entrance and ducked her head.

T-Rex glanced in the direction indicated.

Clay Ellis strutted into the tavern, cocky as hell, sneering at anyone who dared to give a friendly greeting.

"Don't worry. He can't hurt you here," T-Rex said, clenching his fists beneath the table.

"I know. But he can make a fuss." She set down her wineglass. "We can leave now, if you want."

"I'd rather you finished your wine and I finished my beer and neither one of us lets him get to us."

She laughed, though it sounded less than convincing. "You're right." She lifted her glass and sipped. "I shouldn't let him get to me. I'm done with him." As she spoke, she lifted her glass. Her hand shook so much, the wine spilled onto her chest. "Darn. This was my favorite sweater." She dabbed at the stain with her napkin. When that didn't help, she looked up. "I'd better go to the ladies' room and see if I can get this out before it sets."

T-Rex watched as she left their table. His gaze switched from her to where Ellis leaned against the bar, flirting with one of the waitresses trying to fill a drink order.

As far as T-Rex could tell, Ellis hadn't seen Sierra.

"T-Rex, glad we found you." Caveman slipped into the chair Sierra had vacated a minute before. "We've been looking for you."

Kevin Garner, Ghost, Caveman and Hawkeye pulled up chairs around the little table.

"Uh, guys, I'm here with someone."

"Yeah?" Hawkeye, the army ranger of the group of military men, glanced around. "I don't see anyone else."

As one, all four men craned their necks, searching the room.

"Who is she?" Ghost asked. The Navy SEAL smiled, refusing to let T-Rex off the hook.

"Who said it was a she?" T-Rex drummed his fingers on the table, willing the men to leave before Sierra returned.

Caveman laughed. "You, by the way you're avoiding the question." The Delta-Force soldier crossed his arms. These men weren't going to give up until they got an answer.

"It doesn't matter." The only way T-Rex would get rid of them was to find out what they wanted. "What's up?"

"Charlie found the social media site the Free America group moved to," Ghost said. Charlie McClain was an old flame of Ghost's who moonlighted as a cybersnoop for the Department of Homeland Security.

"And?" T-Rex prompted to move the conversation along.

Ghost leaned closer, lowering his voice so that others couldn't hear. "There's been more noise about a potential takeover in the very near future."

"Any dates given?" T-Rex asked.

"No, just a general call to arms to stand ready."

"Great. And we're no closer to figuring out who's involved with the Free America group?"

"Our computer gurus, Hack and Charlie, said that anyone could have set up that group from a public library," Garner said. "The members of the group are using aliases, probably set up on public Wi-Fi systems."

T-Rex's fingers clenched into fists. "How much time do you think we have until they make their move?"

"We've known something was coming for the past couple weeks we've been here," Caveman said.

Garner, the team's leader, shrugged. "It could be a couple more weeks from now, or it could be any day. What did you find at the county records office?"

T-Rex pulled his wallet from his pocket and removed the notepad he'd used to record his notes. Then he brought up the photos of the maps on his cell phone. "Not much more than we already know. Olivia Dawson—" he glanced toward Hawkeye, who'd established a relationship with the woman "—owns this portion of land bordering the current pipeline easement." He pointed to the middle of the map on his phone. "On the north side of the easement is the national park all the way through the mountainous area. East of the Dawson spread, the land was recently sold to Pinnacle Enterprises."

"West of Dawson's ranch is owned by BRE Inc."

"Any idea who BRE Inc. is?" Caveman asked.

Garner's lips thinned. "Bryson Rausch Enterprises."

"The big shot in town?" Ghost asked.

Hawkeye's brows descended. "Liv says Rausch owns half the town. He offered to buy her ranch before her father's casket settled in his grave."

"I can't imagine the man risking a connection to the Free America group," Ghost said. "Why would he? He has plenty of money."

"I can't help but think what's happening with the pipeline is somehow connected with Free America." Garner stared into the distance.

"Wayne Batson admitted he was paid to kill the pipeline inspector," Caveman said.

"But he didn't share the name of the guy who funded him," Ghost reminded them.

"Hack hasn't found the money Batson claims he was paid."

"Unless he was paid in kind." T-Rex's eyes narrowed. "Do you suppose he was paid in weapons?"

"The weapons we can't find?" Caveman asked.

"Yes, those." T-Rex drummed his fingers on the table. "The ones that arrived in the boxes discovered in the Lucky Lou Mine."

Garner nodded, his own eyes narrowing. "Could be."

"We know Batson had a tactical training facility on his property and that he was training individuals there," T-Rex reminded them.

Leaning forward, Garner's eyes narrowed. "We

can only assume they were members of the Free America group and Batson was one of them. But we have no evidence, and Batson didn't keep written or video records of those who came for the training."

"We all surveyed the site," Ghost said. "Watson had mock-ups of several buildings in a group, but we still don't know if they were generic buildings or in the configuration of the planned takeover target."

"We don't have much more than we had when we started." T-Rex slid the notepad over to Garner.

"I'll have Hack check into Pinnacle and continue digging into Rausch's business. He's in the process of reviewing Batson's computer. We hope to glean something from his contacts list."

T-Rex nodded. "What's the plan for tomorrow?"

"We could use some help in the office going through any names Hack comes up with on the contacts list," Garner said.

Ghost raised a hand. "Charlie and I can help."

"I need someone to go interview a man called Leo Fratiani." Garner glanced at T-Rex.

"The other man who offered to purchase Liv's ranch?" T-Rex asked.

"Yes. We need to know his angle," Garner said. "Hack ran a background check on him. He didn't show up on any criminal, military or government databases, but he wants the Dawson place. That makes him a potential for funding Batson's murder of the pipeline inspector."

"Got anything on a Clay Ellis?" T-Rex asked. His attention spun to the bar where Sierra's ex-husband had been standing. He wasn't there. T-Rex sat up straighter, scanning the interior of the tavern.

"I don't have anything on Clay Ellis. Is he a person of interest?" Garner asked.

T-Rex pushed back from the table and stood so fast, his chair fell over backward. "Sorry. I have to go check on someone." He set the chair up straight and hurried toward the restrooms at the back of the tavern.

SIERRA HAD HURRIED to the ladies' room, angry with herself for spilling the wine on her favorite white sweater. She barely made enough money to pay rent, and she hadn't brought all of her clothes from the home she'd shared with Clay. Shortly after she'd left him, he'd told her he'd torched her things in the burning barrel. What she'd packed into the two suitcases was all she had left, all she owned.

Once in the ladies' restroom, she stripped out of her sweater, stuck the wine-stained portion under the faucet and rubbed to get the stain out. Perhaps the spilled wine had been a chance for her to get her act together. Her hands were still shaking uncontrollably. She rubbed the stain harder. She shouldn't let

Clay get to her. They were divorced, and she had a restraining order. All she had to do was call the sheriff and tell him Clay was causing trouble.

The only problem with that scenario was that calling the sheriff had never really helped her situation. Any time she'd fought back against Clay's abuse, it had only made things worse. When she was still married to the man, she had gotten to the point she'd kept her mouth shut and faded into the woodwork.

Well, she'd be darned if she did it anymore. Leaving him had taken all of her willpower at the time. Since she'd been out of his house and on her own, she'd found her own self-worth. She refused to go back to being that coward she'd been for far too long.

She had her back to the door when it swung open.

Embarrassed at being caught standing in her bra, she clutched her sweater to her chest and spun toward the door, an apology on her lips.

Her words froze and her heart ground to a stop. "Clay, what are you doing in here?"

Her ex-husband stood in the doorway, his lip pulled back in a snarl, his dirty blond hair in need of a cut and a good shampoo. His gray eyes narrowed. "Coming to get what belongs to me."

Sierra jammed her arms into the sleeves of the sweater and dragged it over her head. "I don't belong to you, Clay," she said, her tone one of a parent explaining a simple concept to a particularly dense child. Once she had her sweater on, she slung her purse over her shoulder and dug her hand inside.

"You don't have your boyfriend in here to get in the way." He let the door close behind him and stalked her like a snake slithering up to its prey. "What are you going to do?"

"I'll scream."

He shook his head. "Won't do you any good. The band is playing now. No one will hear you." He reached out a hand toward her. "Come with me now and I won't be angry."

Her fingers curled around the hard plastic device T-Rex had armed her with. "I'm not going with you now or ever." She stood straighter, ready to take him on.

"Woman, you're coming with me, one way or another." He grabbed her arm and spun her around, slammed her back into his chest and clamped his arm around her middle.

Holding tightly to the stun gun, Sierra let her purse fall to the floor. "Let go of me, Clay."

"Or what?" He leaned close and whispered into her ear. "You'll yell for your boyfriend?"

"I don't need my boyfriend to fight my battles," she said through gritted teeth as she flicked the on switch.

"That's right. Come along quietly and no one gets hurt."

"No way." And someone was about to get hurt.

"Baby, you belong to me." He edged her toward the door.

Sierra dug in her heels. "I'm not going with you. This is your last warning."

He laughed. "Or what? You can't fight me. You're not strong enough."

"I don't have to be that kind of strong. I just have to be smarter than you. And that's not all that hard." She angled her arm backward and jabbed the stun gun into Clay's thigh.

He screamed like a little girl, shook violently and fell to the floor.

At one time in her life, she might have felt sorry for the man lying on the ground, completely incapacitated. But not anymore.

Sierra waved the stun gun at him. "Don't ever touch me again. Do you hear me?"

He lay there, his eyes wide, his body still twitching.

Flipping her hair back over her shoulders, Sierra tugged her damp sweater into place, picked up her purse off the floor and headed for the door. A woman with brown hair, wearing a leather jacket, stepped in as Sierra stepped out.

Sierra smiled at the brunette's horrified expression. "Don't worry, I'll notify the manager he needs to clean the trash out of the restroom."

The woman's lips twisted. "He must have deserved it."

"You have no idea." With a last glance over her shoulder, Sierra left the restroom and plowed into a wall of muscles.

An iron grip descended on her arms, steadying her.

Shaken, she glanced up into T-Rex's face and sagged against him. "Oh, thank God."

He enveloped her in his strong arms. "What's wrong?"

The woman in the leather jacket who'd walked in while Sierra had walked out pushed out of the ladies' room, shaking her head with a smile as she passed Sierra and T-Rex in the hallway. As the door opened and closed, T-Rex had a chance to see what was inside.

His jaw tightened. "Ellis?"

Sierra held up the stun gun and grinned like the village idiot. "Couldn't have done it without your help. Thank you." She shook all over, but she'd never felt more empowered.

T-Rex caught her wrist, reached up and switched the device to the off position and then chuckled. "Glad it helped." He dropped the device into her handbag. "Are you ready to go?"

"More than ready." She gnawed on her bottom lip. "How long will the effects last again?"

"Sometimes as much as thirty minutes."

"I hate that he will tie up the ladies' restroom for all that time."

"I'll have someone remove him." T-Rex curled his arm around her shoulders and guided her back to the table where his teammates had taken up residence.

Garner stood and held out his hand. "Miss Daniels, it's good to see you again." He frowned. "Is everything all right?"

T-Rex jerked his head toward the hallway. "Can you have someone clean up the dirtbag in the ladies' restroom?"

"Holy hell, did I miss a fight?" Hawkeye jumped up, grinning.

"Miss Daniels had a run-in with her ex-husband, Clay Ellis," T-Rex explained.

"I have a restraining order against him. You can call the sheriff and have him haul Clay out on charges of violating the order," Sierra said. What was the use of a restraining order if the man wasn't punished when he violated it? She'd hit him with a stun gun—how much madder would he get if he was hauled off to jail? Frankly, Sierra didn't care. Clay deserved everything he had coming to him and more.

Garner nodded. "Don't worry about the dirtbag. Just get Miss Daniels home."

"Thank you," Sierra said. For the first time in a long time, she felt like she had others, besides herself, looking out for her. With T-Rex's arm around her, the chill of being caught in the ladies' room by her ex began to fade.

The fact she'd taken care of herself gave her a surge of power, reinforcing her overall decision to get on with her life, without Clay Ellis. She'd been divorced for six months. Perhaps it was time to start dating.

A different kind of warmth spread through her, making her even more aware of the massive marine and the potential she'd felt in his kiss.

Chapter Six

T-Rex walked with Sierra back to the bed-and-breakfast, his arm firmly around her shoulders. He hated that she'd had to face Clay Ellis alone. But his chest swelled with pride over how she'd handled the man. Ellis would think twice before accosting her again.

The sweet day care employee who loved children shouldn't have to put up with an ex-husband of Ellis's low caliber. She deserved someone who could love and respect her. Someone who treated her like the beautiful, caring woman she was.

Someone like him?

He paused in front of her bedroom door and turned to face her. "If you need anything, just yell. The walls aren't very well insulated. I'll hear you."

She laughed. "Not very well insulated?"

Her smile was contagious and had his lips tilting. "You'll see." T-Rex leaned down and brushed a kiss across her forehead. "Sleep tight."

She stood for a long moment, staring up into his eyes.

He counted the seconds, praying she would go inside before he did something he might regret, like kiss her again. Lord knew kissing her a second time would only lead to more internal struggle than he was capable of resisting.

She moved, but not in the direction he expected.

Sierra leaned up on her toes, wrapped her hand around the back of his head and pressed her lips to his. She ended the kiss on a sigh. "I'd ask you in, but I wouldn't want you to think less of me."

"Sweetheart, I wouldn't think less of you. You impress the heck out of me." He leaned his forehead against hers. "The way you handled Ellis in the tavern…" He chuckled. "In my book, that makes you sexy as hell."

He was prolonging something he shouldn't even consider. The walls were thin. Anything they might get into would be heard by all of the guests.

As he thought about it, he couldn't remember seeing any other guests. The rodeo had left town, taking with it all of the out-of-towners, leaving Grizzly Pass feeling empty, almost deserted compared with the rush of people who'd been there days earlier.

Sierra and T-Rex might be the only visitors in the bed-and-breakfast. In which case, why was he worried if noises carried through the wall?

Then again, there was the issue of his being a career marine and confirmed bachelor. He wouldn't feel right playing with Sierra's emotions. She had enough problems dealing with her ex-husband.

"As much as I'd love to come in," he said, "I'm not sure that would be a good idea."

She nodded. "You're probably right. I'm a divorcée with baggage. You really don't want to get involved with me while you're here. Although it's a little late for that. My ex thinks we are already involved. That, I'm sorry to say, will continue to cause you grief while you're in Grizzly Pass."

"I can take care of myself. And the fact you're a divorcée with baggage wasn't what I was thinking about." He brushed a strand of her blond hair back behind her ear. "I don't want to shortchange a beautiful woman who deserves more."

"Shortchange?"

He nodded, traced his thumb across her lip and resisted kissing where his thumb had been. "I'm only here for another week, maybe two or three. But then I'll return to my unit. I won't start anything I can't finish."

"Oh, I wasn't thinking of any commitment. I was thinking of practice." Her cheeks reddened.

He frowned. "Practice?"

"I haven't been on a date since high school. Spending time with you is like being on a date. I could use the practice." She laid her hand on his chest and stared at her fingers, not into his eyes. "I wouldn't expect you to stick around. And when you leave, I promise not to be heartbroken." Her voice softened, fading away with the last word.

He couldn't resist, he had to kiss her. She was too beautiful when she was embarrassed. T-Rex bent and skimmed his mouth across hers.

She lifted her chin and forced the connection to be more than a brief touch. Her other hand rose to cup the back of his head.

There was no going back. He crushed her body to his, the evidence of his desire pressing against her soft belly.

After plundering her mouth, he dragged his lips across her chin to suck her earlobe between his teeth. "This is insane," he whispered.

Sierra tilted her head to the side, giving him better access to her ear and to her neck. "Completely," she responded, in a breathy voice, curling her leg behind his.

Holy hell, what was he thinking? This woman was too recently divorced. If he took her now, he'd be taking advantage of her when she was at her most vulnerable.

Though he wanted to swing her up into his arms and carry her into the bedroom, he fought that urge, broke the kiss and took a step back. He breathed in short, tight breaths, clenching his fists to keep from taking her back into his arms.

She stood in front of him, her lips swollen from his kiss, her chest rising and falling as quickly as his. "I'm sorry."

"Why?" he asked.

"I must have done something wrong." She shook her head, her eyes glassy, a pucker on her forehead.

"You didn't do anything wrong. I'm the one who almost screwed up." He took her key from her and slid it into the doorknob. "Go to bed, Sierra. Sleep. I don't want to be your next mistake. Save yourself for a better guy who'll stick around."

Before she could say another word, he angled her through the door and closed it between them. It had to be one of the hardest things he'd ever had to do.

With leaden steps and tight jeans, he continued down the hallway to his room, entered, closed the door behind him and leaned against it. What had he been thinking?

Sierra Daniels was strictly off-limits. She'd been abused, for heaven's sake. Freshly divorced and vulnerable, she would only be hurt if he made love to her. As much as she tried to convince him that she needed "practice," she needed a lot more than that. She needed to learn to love herself before she loved another. Not that he was anyone to give ad-

vice on love and romance. He was one big failure
in that arena.

Pushing away from the door, he grabbed his shaving kit and a towel and headed across the hall to
the shared bathroom. A cold shower would help to
douse the raging desire that had almost cost him
his control.

Ten minutes later, he climbed out of the shower,
dried off and wrapped his towel around his waist.
With his shaving kit in hand, he walked out of the
bathroom and almost ran over Sierra bent over in the
hallway, collecting from the floor an array of shampoo and conditioner bottles and a tube of toothpaste.

"Sorry, I'll get out of your way." She shoved all
the items into a torn plastic bag, gathered them to
her chest and finally glanced up.

Her gaze started at his shins and climbed to the
towel, pausing at the tent his instant desire had created.

T-Rex groaned. He'd need thirty minutes more
in an ice bath to tamp down the intense heat that
exploded inside when Sierra's gaze swept upward.

What sweet hell was this? He gripped her elbow
and brought her to her feet. "Are you okay?"

"I'm fine," she said, her cheeks bright red.

"Good, because now I'm not." He turned her toward the bathroom and gave her a gentle nudge. "Go,
before I forget how to be a gentleman."

SIERRA STAGGERED INTO the bathroom. The door closed behind her and she finally remembered to inhale. Then her breaths came in ragged gasps. She pressed a hand to her chest, willing her heartbeat to slow.

Seeing T-Rex in nothing but a towel had taken her breath away. The man had the broadest, most anatomically perfect chest of any man she'd ever seen in person or on television. But the evidence of his desire had captured her attention, shoving every other thought completely out of her head. He'd been hard for her.

Before she'd headed for the bathroom, Sierra had gone to her room, her hormones hopping, her libido so stimulated she hadn't been able to settle into a chair or in bed. She'd wandered around the room, counting the number of steps it took to get from one side to the other.

After ten laps, she'd forced herself to sit at the little desk and dump out the contents of her purse. She rearranged them and placed them back in the different compartments, assigning a specific pouch for the stun gun. She didn't want to waste time hunting for it the next time she needed to defend herself.

Once she'd completed her inventory and re-packing of the items in her purse, she turned on the television in the corner and flipped through the channels. Nothing had appealed to her, or taken her mind off the man in the room next to hers. She turned off the television, grabbed the plastic grocery bag of toiletries she'd brought with her from her apartment, panties and a nightgown and headed for the bathroom across the hall.

She'd almost reached the door when the bottom fell out of the bag, spilling her shampoo, conditioner, lotion and toothpaste onto the floor. She'd dropped to pick them up when the bathroom door opened and… and… Sweet heaven, T-Rex had stood in front of her.

Standing in the bathroom he'd vacated, Sierra burned with the heat of her desire. Never in her life had she been that strongly attracted to any man. Not even during the early days of dating Clay. Yes, there had been a mild form of lust. But this was something entirely different. The feeling consumed her and made her lose focus on everything else.

Sierra shook herself, set her things on the counter and stripped out of her clothes, determined to push the man out of her thoughts. No man should have that much control over her thoughts and imagination. It could only lead to heartache and losing herself once again. She'd come too far in her self-realization to backslide now.

In the shower, she scrubbed her hair, face and body, trying to ignore the sensitivity of her nipples and the ache between her legs. She would not succumb to her desire.

T-Rex had laid it out for her. He wasn't staying. And he hadn't invited her to leave when he left. Not that he should. They were strangers, having known each other for only a few short hours.

She rinsed the suds out of her hair and turned the shower to its coolest setting. Anything to chill the heat inside her body. If she didn't get a grasp on her physical reactions to the man, she'd never get any sleep.

Dressed in her nightgown, her hair wrapped turban-style in the towel, she eased open the door. The hallway was clear. A stab of disappointment assailed her.

"Idiot," she muttered beneath her breath. "Like he'd be interested in you. And you shouldn't be interested in him."

The door across the hall opened and T-Rex stood in the frame, wearing jeans and nothing else. "Did you say something?"

Her cheeks flamed. "No, just talking to myself." She scurried for her door. "You weren't kidding about paper-thin walls, were you?"

He chuckled. "No, I wasn't. The couple who'd been in the room on the other side of me were very loud in their lovemaking. I had a hard time facing them in the morning."

"Well, you don't have to worry about me. I won't be making a whole lot of noise," she babbled. "I don't think I snore, and once I'm out, I don't get up for anything short of a fire alarm."

"Good to know." His gaze swept her from her head to her bare feet, his eyes flaring as he skimmed over her bare knees and calves. "Good night."

His glance warmed her from the inside, spreading heat to her chest and lower to the juncture of her thighs.

"Yes, good night." She rushed through her door and closed it before she did something stupid like falling into the big marine's arms and begging him to make love to her. Wow, he had charisma in spades. How did women resist?

With little hope of sleep, she lay on the bed. The headboard rested against the wall she shared with T-Rex. If the walls were as thin as he'd said, he could hear her if she cried out.

After Clay had attacked her twice that day, Sierra felt more reassured having T-Rex on the other side of the wall. And she had the stun gun, should she need it.

For a long time, she lay in the dark, staring up at the ceiling. Sleep eluded her. She found herself listening for sounds from the other room, wondering if T-Rex was having trouble sleeping, too. The next thought that popped into her head was the big question: Did he sleep in pajamas or in the nude?

Sierra moaned, rolled onto her side and punched

her pillow. This was not going to work. Thinking of a naked man would not put her to sleep anytime soon.

"Everything okay in there?" a deep, resonant voice said from the other side of the wall.

Sierra yelped and sat up.

"Sorry," he said. "I didn't mean to frighten you. I heard you moan and thought maybe you weren't feeling well."

Flopping over onto her back, Sierra pulled the extra pillow up into her arms and hugged it. "Good Lord, I can hear you as if you were in my room."

He chuckled. "Told you."

"You really must have gotten a blow-by-blow account of the couple's nights."

"Pun intended?"

It was Sierra's turn to chuckle. "If it fits…"

Quiet settled in again, but Sierra couldn't relax. It was as if she were clinging to an edge, waiting for another word from T-Rex to pull her back. When he didn't say anything, she couldn't remain silent. "Why did you join the military?"

"To get out of Texas and see the world." He snorted. "Only it turns out that it's not always the best part of the world."

"I can imagine." She picked at the pillowcase. "I know you said you're not married, but have you ever been?"

"No."

"You're a…good-looking guy. How have you gone all these years without getting hitched?" She bit her lip. "Sorry. If I'm being too nosy, just tell me to shove off."

"No. It's okay," he said. "First of all, I haven't met anyone who could put up with me."

Sierra laughed. "I find that hard to believe."

"It's true. I'm stubborn, cranky and hard to get along with on a good day."

"I get along fine with you."

"Second, after my first couple of deployments, watching other guys who had wives back home, I couldn't see myself subjecting a woman to the hardship of being married to a career military man. Many of my men would return to empty houses—their wives having moved back to their mamas, taking the kids with them."

"Some women are a lot stronger than you think. Surely you could find one who would be there when you got back."

"Yeah. *If* I got back." His voice faded to little more than a whisper. "Or *if* I came back in one piece."

Sierra's chest tightened. She could hear the strain in his tone. "What do you mean?"

"I wouldn't want to come back in a body bag. Or worse, a paraplegic. What woman wants to take care of her children and her husband for the rest of her life?"

"A woman who loves him more than life," Sierra answered.

"I couldn't put a woman through the heartache and demands of a life caring for an invalid."

Another long silence stretched between them.

Sierra broke it with, "You know someone like this, don't you?"

His answer was in the form of more silence.

"I'm sorry," Sierra said. "It must hurt to see one of your men so badly injured."

"Hurts even more that I can do nothing to make it better." T-Rex's voice was tight and hard. "He'll never walk again. He'll never throw a ball for his son. He'll never feel the softness of his wife's skin."

Tears welled in Sierra's eyes. "And because of this, you will never marry?"

"Yes," he said, his tone harsh.

"Did you ever think that maybe a woman would want to make the choice, to be the one to decide whether or not to take the risk on you?"

"It doesn't matter," he said. "I'd rather die than be a burden on a woman."

"Sometimes you aren't given a choice. Your friend was given that choice. I'm sure his wife would rather have him alive than not."

"I told you I was terrible boyfriend material."

"Again, you weren't lying. Not because you're a member of the military. Most women can deal with that. You're terrible boyfriend material because you won't give a woman the opportunity to decide for herself if she's ready and willing to take the risk on you. You just avoid the situation altogether."

"Yes. Exactly."

"In the meantime, you're alone." Sierra's heart contracted. One of the reasons she'd stayed with her husband as long as she had was because she was terrible at being alone. Perhaps the death of her parents had made her less secure in her solitude. For the past few months of being single, she'd learned being alone wasn't all that bad. But she wouldn't want to be alone forever.

"I like being alone," T-Rex said.

"Because you've been alone for so long you don't remember what it's like to have someone else to share your life."

"I have my unit."

"And they are with you 24/7 when you're deployed, but they go home to their families when you're Stateside. Which leaves you alone again."

"I like it," he insisted.

"Uh-huh."

"I can choose what to eat for dinner. I don't have to ask permission if I want to go to a movie, and I can walk around my apartment naked, if I like."

Sierra laughed. "Yeah, but you don't have anyone to talk to when you're down or someone with whom you can share the beauty of a sunset."

"I don't need any of that."

"No?" Sierra leaned up on her elbows. "What about children? Don't you want children of your own? A little girl or a miniature T-Rex to teach how to play ball?"

"No." His tone was hard and final. "What happens if I did have a little boy, and then I came back a paraplegic like Gunny? What then? My son wouldn't have a father to teach him the things a father is supposed to."

"Your Gunny is alive. He will be there for his son, to teach him by his words. He can hire a coach. I'm sure his son would rather have him than no father at all."

"I won't do that to any kid of mine. War's hell. I won't put a woman through the uncertainty. I won't have her waiting for the dreaded call or visit from the chaplain."

"If you love someone enough, you'll take whatever time you're given with that person," Sierra said softly.

"You've been reading too many romance novels. I'm surprised you still believe in love, given the fact you're divorced."

Sierra flinched and hugged the pillow harder, her

eyes stinging. His words hurt. "For a long time, I thought I was the one who'd failed at my marriage. I stopped believing in love. It couldn't be real. It was just lust, and when that faded, you had nothing." Tears welled in her eyes. Those had been dark days in which she'd felt more hopeless than at any other time of her life.

"Look, Sierra, I'm sorry. I shouldn't have said what I said about your divorce."

"No, you're right. It took being away from Clay to realize it wasn't me. *He* wasn't capable of loving me. And maybe I wasn't capable of loving him. But I know I'm capable of love, and I'm not giving up on finding it." She held up her hand, even though he couldn't see it. "Don't worry. I won't look for it in you. You've been very clear on the subject. Now, if you don't mind, I'm tired and I have to get some sleep."

Silence filled the gloom, making it seem even gloomier.

"Good night, Sierra. I hope you find it."

I hope you do, too, she thought. *Then, you'll understand.*

Chapter Seven

T-Rex tossed and turned through the night. Sierra's words stuck with him, making it hard for him to clear his mind. For a woman who'd been in an abusive relationship, she was still optimistic about finding love.

As morning light edged through the curtains, T-Rex gave up on sleep, put on his running shoes and sweats and went out for a jog. Whenever he needed to think, he ran. He had a lot to think about, and there didn't seem to be enough time or road to ponder everything on his mind.

Number one was the last bit of conversation he'd had with Sierra. No matter how hard he tried to push it to the back of his mind, he couldn't. The last thing he needed to be thinking about was love. He was married to the corps. He was first, and foremost, a marine.

Any woman who dared to fall in love with a career marine was setting herself up for heartache and sacrifice. She would be left alone more often than not. Any children from the relationship would be raised by their mother. Deployments were a given, and they could be as long as fourteen months at a time. Gunny had missed more birthdays and dance recitals than he'd managed to attend. What kind of life was that for a woman, or children, for that matter?

Then why were so many of his troops married? Sure, some had deployed to come back to an empty house, their wives picking up and moving the kids back to their mamas. But there were those who kept the home fires burning and greeted their loved ones when they stepped off the planes. They were there with love in their eyes, truly happy to see their husbands.

Why couldn't that be him?

An image came to his mind of Sierra waiting at the airport or on the tarmac of a military landing strip, her blue eyes alight with happy tears, a pretty little girl, with her blond hair and blue eyes standing beside her, clutching her hand.

His heart pinched in his chest, forcing him to slow to a walk. He'd seen wives like that with their little ones gathered around their legs. Waiting for their husbands and fathers to step off the plane. The happy reunions always made him rethink his stance on his own bachelorhood.

Then he'd see a casket unloaded from the bowels

of a plane, the widow and children of the fallen marine there to meet the transfer detail with the hearse.

No matter how much he longed for the love and comfort of having someone waiting for him at home, T-Rex couldn't do it. He wouldn't put a woman through that kind of heartache. He picked up the pace until he was running again. Anyone who would go willingly into a relationship with a career marine had to either be so in love to the point she couldn't think straight, or just insane. The worry alone would age the one left behind.

Again, he thought of Sierra, who still believed in love, despite having escaped an abusive husband. She deserved a man who would go to work and come home each day. A man whose job wasn't to kill, and in the process be shot at, have bombs lobbed in his direction or IEDs explode beneath his feet. She deserved an accountant, banker or rancher. A man who would always be there for her, who would always be home at night to protect her.

The thought of someone else coming home to Sierra made T-Rex's heart pinch even tighter. He pushed past the irritating pain and ran even faster. By the time he was almost back to the bed-and-breakfast, he was running full out. No amount of physical exertion was enough to push thoughts of Sierra from his mind. He might have to move out of the bed-and-breakfast to get away from her and the attraction he was feeling toward her.

As the bed-and-breakfast came into view, he slowed, winding down from the punishing pace. Whatever he did, he had to stay away from Sierra Daniels. She was everything he wanted but couldn't have. The sooner he accepted that, the better off he'd be.

Mrs. McCall was awake and setting the table in the shared dining room.

"Good morning, Mrs. McCall."

She glanced up with a smile. "Good morning, Mr. Trainor. You're up early."

"Yes, ma'am." He didn't bother to inform her that he couldn't sleep because of one blond-haired, blue-eyed beauty on the other side of the wall of his bedroom. What good would it do?

Mrs. McCall laid out another napkin and placed a knife and fork on it. "How do you like your eggs cooked? And how many?"

"Two, over easy, and a slice of toast."

"Coffee?"

"Yes, ma'am. Black."

"It'll be ready in ten minutes. Just enough time for you to get a shower." She winked. "Would you happen to know when Miss Daniels will be awake?"

And why would Mrs. McCall think he'd know

Miss Daniels's hours? Had she heard them kissing and talking?

"I'm awake," a soft voice said from the top of the staircase.

T-Rex's pulse stuttered and then raced as he turned to face the woman who'd been on his mind nonstop since he'd closed his eyes in an attempt to sleep last night.

Sierra descended the steps, her hand trailing along the rail. She wore a form-hugging light blue knit blouse the color of her eyes and a navy blue skirt. Her long, slender legs were encased in dark navy tights, emphasizing her tight calves and narrow ankles. She had her long blond hair loose around her shoulders.

The overall effect left T-Rex breathless, the desire he'd hoped he'd run off surging back in full force. "I'll go shower," he said through tight lips. He passed her as she took the last step down.

For a brief instant, their gazes connected.

T-Rex felt as if he'd been blasted by a bolt of lightning when he looked into her eyes.

Her irises flared, and she caught her bottom lip between her teeth.

Swallowing a groan, T-Rex jerked his glance away from hers and stumbled on the first step. Cursing softly beneath his breath, he caught himself.

Sierra touched his arm. "Are you all right?"

"I'm fine," he forced out, his arm on fire where her hand lay. He was freakin' great. The one person he needed to avoid was touching him, and he was going hot all over like a teenager in lust. Tearing himself away, he started up the steps.

"Is there anything I can do to help?" Sierra said behind him.

"Yes, thank you," Mrs. McCall responded. "If you could finish setting the table, I'll start cooking. How many eggs would you like and how do you like them cooked?"

"Two eggs, over easy, and a piece of toast would be nice, thank you."

Halfway up the staircase, T-Rex stubbed his toe on the riser in front of him. Had Sierra heard him order his eggs, or did she truly like hers just like his?

"Did you hear that, Mr. Trainor?" Mrs. McCall called out. "Just like you. You're making this easy. You're two peas in a pod."

T-Rex said something inane and continued up the stairs.

"Coffee or tea?" Mrs. McCall was asking.

"Coffee, definitely. Black," Sierra said in her soft voice.

At the top of the stairs now, T-Rex groaned. Could the woman be any more perfect? If she was a Denver Broncos fan, he might as well throw in the towel and ask her to marry him.

AFTER A RESTLESS night of very little sleep, Sierra had promised she wouldn't let herself get all wrapped up in T-Rex that morning. She'd been thankful she had the bathroom all to herself, without bumping into the man. If she was honest with herself, she had been a little disappointed that she hadn't seen him.

Determined to wipe him from her mind and get on with her life, she'd left her bedroom, ready to make it a wonderful day spending time with the children at the community center. Working with children always took her mind off her own troubles and made her smile.

Then she'd seen T-Rex at the bottom of the stairs, and all bets were off. He was right back front and center in her thoughts. Not that he'd ever left them. And he was all sweaty, his face and muscular arms glistening in the dining room lights.

Sierra's heart skipped several beats and butterflies fluttered in her belly. She could feel last night's kiss tingling on her lips.

And when she'd touched him… Holy hell, she was going to be sorely disappointed when the man left Grizzly Pass. She hadn't felt this excited by any man. Ever. Not even when she'd first started dating the captain of the football team in high school. That had been back when Clay was at the top of his game. He'd been nice to her and treated her like he really cared. She'd been flattered and thought she was in love with him.

But never had she felt the spark T-Rex set off in her by merely touching her.

As she set flatware on the dining room table, she listened for the sound of the water running in the shower upstairs and imagined T-Rex naked.

He'd told her not to get attached. And she had no intention of doing so. But what would it hurt to have a fling with the man? Sierra shivered and her core heated in anticipation of getting naked with T-Rex and making love.

He'd be so powerful in bed. All those muscles would be hers to touch, if only for a night. Then perhaps she'd get him out of her system and move on to finding a man she could fall in love with and who would fall in love with her.

She finished laying out the silverware and napkins and helped Mrs. McCall by bringing the toast and an insulated carafe of coffee to the table.

Mrs. McCall smiled. "Thank you for helping. The eggs are almost ready. I'll bring them out in a minute. Why don't you make yourself comfortable in the dining room?"

Sierra wandered out to the dining room. She couldn't hear the sound of water running. Her senses perked and her pulse sped. T-Rex would be down soon, and they would have to sit at the same table for breakfast.

How should she act? How could she look at him and not show how very attracted she was to him? Taking a deep breath, she purposely turned away from the staircase. She would not let T-Rex or any other man have that profound an effect on her. Letting her breath out slowly, she paused to stare out the window as the morning sun bathed the trees and other houses along the street in light. If she concentrated on the beauty of the world around her, instead of the marine in the shower upstairs, she might make it through breakfast without drooling.

The weatherman had predicted the morning would be clear and sunny. Later that evening clouds would roll in from the west. For now, the sunshine filled Sierra with a feeling of hope, and hope was a good thing when you were divorced, dirt-poor and somewhat homeless while your apartment was being reroofed.

A dark pickup pulled up to the curb on the other side of the street.

As if a cloud descended on her spirits, the hope Sierra had felt faded, replaced by a heavy pall of anger and dread. "Damn him," she whispered, her hands shaking as she stepped back from the window.

Arms came up around her and a deep voice asked, "What's wrong?"

Sierra spun in T-Rex's arms and pressed her cheek against his chest. "Out there," she said, refusing to look again.

T-Rex stiffened. "Ellis." He gripped her arms and set her away from him. "I'll take care of him."

"No. Let the sheriff. I have a restraining order against him. If he gets any closer than fifty feet, the sheriff can arrest him."

"He's harassing you."

"He never liked to lose." Sierra stared up into T-Rex's face. "I'll call the sheriff."

"Do it. And if they don't show up and he's still there when we're finished with breakfast, I'll have words with him."

She smiled and touched his arm. "You don't have to fight my battles for me."

"Ellis doesn't have to harass you."

"Now that I have the stun gun, I can take care of myself." She stepped away and pulled her cell phone from her purse. As she hit the number for the sheriff's department, she left the dining room and entered the front living area.

"Sheriff's department," a woman's voice answered.

"This is Sierra Daniels. Is Sheriff Scott available?"

"One moment, please."

After a short pause, a deep, masculine voice came

through the receiver. "Sierra, Sheriff Scott here. What's up?"

She sighed. "Clay's at it again."

"When is that boy going to get it through his thick head you aren't going back to him?"

"I don't know. But he's parked outside Mrs. McCall's bed-and-breakfast, where I'm staying. I didn't call, but I had two altercations with him yesterday."

"Sierra, you did right. We'll do something about it."

"I know. I just need to remember to call."

"That's right. We're here to help. I'll send a unit by," Sheriff Scott said.

"Thank you."

"Are you going to be okay?"

Sierra glanced across the two rooms at T-Rex standing by the window, staring out at her ex-husband. "Yes. I'm okay. I can protect myself. I just don't want him hanging around and scaring my landlady."

"We'll take care of it."

Sierra ended the call and joined T-Rex in the dining room.

Mrs. McCall entered, carrying their plates of steaming eggs.

As they settled in for their breakfast, Mrs. McCall asked, "Would you mind if I put the news on the television?"

"Not at all," Sierra answered.

"I'd like that," said T-Rex.

The bed-and-breakfast owner hit the remote for the fifty-inch television mounted on the wall in the corner of the dining room. She gave them a sassy smile as she adjusted the volume. "I love my big television. I occasionally open the dining room during football season. I love my Denver Broncos."

"I was here during your airing of the last playoff game." Sierra said. "The food was great, and the company was so much fun." It had been shortly after her divorce. She'd dared to venture out by herself and had thoroughly enjoyed the football game. "I'm a huge Broncos fan, too."

Beside her, T-Rex choked on his coffee.

"Are you all right?" she asked.

He set the cup down and covered his mouth. "Wrong pipe."

Mrs. McCall tuned in to the news station based out of Jackson Hole, Wyoming, the closest station to Grizzly Pass. "Look, there's Grady Morris on the steps of the state capitol."

"Isn't he the guy who was here a few days ago, campaigning for state senator?"

Mrs. McCall nodded. "He's been campaigning all over the state. The elections aren't far off and the incumbent is getting old, but he is a favorite." She turned up the volume.

A woman in a gray skirt suit raised her hand. "Mr.

Morris, what's your stance on global warming? Will you vote for legislation to reduce greenhouse gases?"

The candidate stood straight, his gaze on the gathered crowd more than the female reporter asking the question. "I will study the situation and make the best possible decisions based on the scientific findings and what my constituents want."

"Great way to avoid the question," Sierra muttered.

"What about the pipeline running through the state and the southern border of Yellowstone National Park?" A dark-haired man, wearing a dark jacket, held out a microphone. "Will you put pressure on the federal government to put a stop to further expansion of the pipeline access?"

"I will stand by the people and do what's in the best interest of the people of Wyoming," Morris responded.

"Another nonanswer," Sierra noted.

"Is it true, Mr. Morris, that you were once on the Transcontinental Pipeline Inc. board of directors?"

Morris nodded, brows dipping. "Your point?"

"And isn't it true Transcontinental bought out Rocky Mountain Pipeline?"

Again, Morris nodded, his eyes narrowing slightly.

"And isn't Transcontinental in the process of negotiating their existing contract for the maintenance of the pipeline through Wyoming and for additional pipelines to pass, as well?"

"I wouldn't know," Morris responded. "I haven't been on the board for nearly seven years. Next question, please." Morris looked at the others in the crowd.

"Is it true Transcontinental is being investigated for failure to provide sufficient maintenance to the existing pipelines?" The man in the dark jacket wasn't going to let go of the pipeline angle.

Morris's mouth thinned into a straight line. "I'll take other questions from other reporters now."

The woman in the gray suit held up her hand.

Morris nodded to her.

"Mr. Morris, I'd like to know the answer to the other reporter's question. Is Transcontinental being investigated for failure to provide sufficient maintenance to the existing pipeline?"

"If they are, it should be available as public record." Morris straightened his suit coat and stepped down from the top step at the capitol. "If you'll excuse me, I have work to do."

"Mr. Morris, if Transcontinental hasn't been maintaining the pipeline properly, are the people of Wyoming in danger of a pipeline rupturing?"

"I don't have the answer to that question," he responded.

The woman in the gray suit followed Morris as

he attempted to push through the crowd of reporters. "Will you, as a senator, make certain all measures are taken to protect the people of your state from a potentially disastrous situation with the pipeline?"

Morris didn't respond. The woman in gray turned to her cameraman. "There seems to be more than meets the eye on Grady Morris's connection to the Transcontinental Pipeline. I'll bring you my findings in the evening news." She signed off and the news returned to the station and the weather report.

"Mr. Morris has an uphill battle if he plans to be the next senator of Wyoming," Mrs. McCall said. "Too many people are unhappy about the pipeline running through our state to begin with. If Morris is in any way connected with the pipeline shenanigans, he won't get the votes he needs. And if Transcontinental thinks they'll put another one in with the first, they have another think coming. Ever since they bought out Rocky Mountain Pipeline, they've laid off everyone and quit maintaining the line. I'd be surprised if they don't get fined and booted off the pipeline altogether." Mrs. McCall grimaced. "Sorry. I'll step down from my soapbox now." She finished her tea and stood. "Can I get you anything? More coffee? Tea?"

Sierra held up her hand. "I'm full. Breakfast was great. If you keep cooking like that, I might decide to live here even after they finish the renovations on my apartment building."

"Sweetie, you're always welcome here. You're practically family."

"Thank you, Mrs. McCall." Sierra gathered her plate and stood.

Mrs. McCall paused on her way to the kitchen, staring through the window. "Now, what is the sheriff doing on our street so early in the morning?" She left the dining room and pushed through the swinging door into the kitchen.

Sierra's pulse sped up. She deliberately stopped beside T-Rex and piled his plate on top of hers. As she passed the window, she could see a sheriff's car pulled up against the curb where Clay's truck had been a few minutes before.

A smile curled her lips, and she felt a hundred pounds lighter. "Clay's gone," Sierra said.

"Even so, I'm following you to the community center today." T-Rex pushed back from the table and gathered the glasses.

"You don't have to," Sierra reminded him.

He shook his head. "No, but I want to. Can we not argue about it this morning?"

She twisted her lips in a wry grin. "Deal. And thanks." The smile he gave her spread warmth throughout her body.

And so, she had her escort to the community

center. Clay wasn't there waiting to harass her, but Brenda was driving up as she arrived, and by the stupid grin on her face, she wasn't likely to let Sierra by without some good-natured ribbing.

Sierra hugged herself around her middle as she walked into the building. The man made her feel cared about and protected. No amount of ribbing would knock the smile off her face.

Chapter Eight

T-Rex waited until Sierra was inside the community center before he left. He didn't like leaving her with the possibility of Ellis showing up again and making a nuisance of himself. But he couldn't be there all the time for her. He had a job to do.

Just to relieve some of his anxiety, he stopped at the sheriff's office.

Sheriff Scott was standing at the front desk, talking to a deputy, when T-Rex entered. He finished what he was saying and turned with his hand outstretched and a smile on his face. "Mr. Trainor. Good morning. What can I do for you?"

T-Rex gripped the man's hand. "I wanted to thank you for sending a unit by the bed-and-breakfast this morning."

The sheriff's smile faded, and he released T-Rex's hand. "Clay Ellis needs a swift kick in the backside. The man can't get it through his thick, mean head that things were over between him and Ms. Daniels the day the judge granted her divorce."

T-Rex nodded. "That's the reason I'm here. I'm worried he'll try something."

The sheriff chuckled. "I heard from my guys that she got him good with a stun gun last night at the tavern. When he came out of it, he was madder than a wet hen."

"That's what I'm afraid of," T-Rex said. "He might see it as a challenge to catch her when her guard is down."

"You're right. I'll have a unit swing by the community center every hour during the day to make sure she's okay."

"Thanks."

"You and your team getting any closer to figuring out who's responsible for all the troubles around here lately?"

"We have bits and pieces, but not the full picture."

"That's about where we are. We think we know some of the players in the Free America group, but we don't have enough evidence to get the county judge to issue search warrants. Besides, we doubt they'd keep their weapons and plans in their houses. There are enough caves and old mines in those mountains to keep us looking for a very long time."

"Agreed."

"Well, keep us informed." Sheriff Scott clapped a hand to T-Rex's back. "We're here to help each other."

"You bet." T-Rex left the sheriff's office. He made his way to the Blue Moose Tavern and climbed the stairs on the outside to the temporary office of the Safe Haven operations center.

Ghost, Caveman and Hawkeye were at the conference table, staring at a map.

Garner stood behind Hack at the array of computer monitors. "Good, now that we're all here, we can get to work."

"What's the plan for the day?" T-Rex asked.

Their temporary boss pointed to two of the men. "Ghost and Caveman will continue to interview neighbors and friends of Don Sweeney to see if anyone saw other people coming and going from the man's apartment. Hopefully someone will come up with the name of the man who hired Sweeney to kill Olivia Dawson's father."

Sweeney had admitted he'd been paid to murder the rancher who owned the land bordering the pipeline. They still didn't know who'd paid him or if he had connections to Free America.

"I'd like to check Wayne Batson's place," Hawkeye said. "I feel like the sheriff might have missed something. The man trained people for combat, for heaven's sake. He's bound to have a bunker of weapons hidden somewhere on his ranch."

"I can help with the search," T-Rex offered.

Garner shook his head. "I have other plans for you. And I need to coordinate the search of Batson's ranch with the sheriff. They have the authority to search the ranch. No use getting hit with trespassing charges."

"After Caveman and Ms. Saunders were hunted like animals on Batson's ranch—" Hawkeye frowned "—I'd say we have a right to be there."

Garner nodded. "Still, we need to coordinate with the sheriff. If he has people out there, you don't want to surprise them. With everything that's happened lately, they might shoot first and ask questions later. Not to mention the folks Batson trained on his ranch. They could still be using his facilities without our knowledge."

Unfortunately, Batson's computer information concerning people who'd been through his training camp had been programmed to self-destruct when tampered with. As soon as Hack had made his first attempt, the system shut him out and initiated a program to delete data files. Hack had turned off the server as soon as he'd realized what had happened. At that point the server had been sent to the state crime lab in the hope they could recover the data.

In the meantime, a shipment of approximately thirty AR-15, military-grade rifles had been sent to someone in the area. And they had yet to discover their whereabouts. Thirty semiautomatic rifles would do a lot of damage in a takeover.

Garner turned to T-Rex. "I have a special assignment for you. Today, I want you to tail Leo Fratiani. Our searches online haven't turned up much of anything. Find out if he's really on the up and up."

"Will do," T-Rex said.

Garner continued, "Then, this afternoon, I have a friend from the Wyoming Army National Guard flying in with a UH-60 Black Hawk helicopter. I need you to be available when he gets here. He'll take you up to scout the hills and valleys along and around the pipeline. Perhaps what we can't see from the ground, you can see from the air."

"I would think you'd want to be in that chopper," T-Rex noted.

"I do. Major Bailey and Lieutenant Strohm are on loan for the afternoon to get some flying time in. Unfortunately, I have an online meeting scheduled with my higher headquarters this afternoon that I can't miss. My boss wants a status on what's happening here in Grizzly Pass." Garner's lips thinned. "I'd like to tell him we've identified all of the members of Free America and found the person who funded the purchase of the AR-15s. As you all know, we're not there."

The men around the table were silent. If the others

were like T-Rex, they took it personally that they hadn't found the source of the problems.

"We don't know if the troubles are directly related to the pipeline, or if someone is trying to throw us off." Garner turned away from the team and paced the length of the room and back. "The heavily armed Free America faction could be the real issue here. We know about the AR-15s, but we don't know what else they might have gotten their hands on. The sooner we locate the weapons cache and get a list of the people involved, the sooner we nail the ones responsible, and you can go back to your units."

"We're on it," T-Rex said.

Ghost nodded. "We want this resolved as badly as you. I'm from this area. I hate seeing it threatened."

"If Free America stages a takeover, anyone could be at risk. Look what happened to the local children. That was bad enough," Caveman said. "A nice old man was murdered, and all of those children could have died in that abandoned mine."

"Precisely why we can't let this drag on any longer. And with the internet hopping with Free America activity and forewarnings, we need to make it happen soon." Garner clapped his hands together. "Let's get to it."

Ghost, Caveman and Hawkeye left the office. Garner lagged behind. "Fratiani is staying at the Heartland Hotel. He likes to take his breakfast at the diner and eat lunch and dinner at the Blue Moose Tavern. What he does with the rest of his day, we don't know. He drives out of town."

"What's he look like?" T-Rex asked.

Garner turned to the man in the corner. "Hack?"

The computer guru had been sitting quietly, tapping away at his keyboard. He tapped some more, and an image popped up on one of his monitors of a man with dark hair and dark eyes.

"This is from his driver's license from the state of California."

"He's not even from Wyoming?" T-Rex stepped up behind Hack.

"No. He approached Olivia Dawson stating he was interested in purchasing her property, Stone Oak Ranch, for an investor. My inquiries indicate he works for a company called LF Enterprises. He's listed as the owner."

"Is he a broker?" T-Rex asked.

Hack nodded. "I looked up his license in the state of California. It's current and relatively new. He's also a licensed financial adviser. Also recent. Prior to those certifications, he worked for the pipeline industry."

"Okay, he probably knows his stuff and might have an inside track on the pipeline dealings." T-Rex faced Garner again. "Do you want me to interview him, or tail him and observe covertly?"

Garner had joined him behind Hack. "I'd rather he didn't know you were on to him. If he's up to something, you might have a better chance of discovering what it is, if he doesn't know you're following him."

T-Rex nodded. "Will do." As he left the office and descended the stairs, he checked his watch. It was still early. He might catch Fratiani at the diner.

T-Rex hopped into his truck and drove the few blocks to the diner, got out and went in. It didn't take long to spot the man he was to follow that day.

Fratiani looked much like the picture on his driver's license, with his dark hair and dark eyes. He sat alone at a table with a cup of coffee, an empty plate and his cell phone in his hand.

T-Rex ordered a cup of coffee to go and sat at the counter mixing a dash of sugar and cream in the cup, though he preferred it black. He sipped the steaming brew and glanced over the rim of the cup.

About that time, Fratiani threw a twenty on the table and got up.

T-Rex gave him enough time to exit the building before he capped his coffee and followed.

The broker climbed into a four-wheel-drive Jeep and backed out of his parking space, holding his cell phone to his ear. He headed south out of town.

T-Rex jumped into his truck, settled the coffee in a cup holder and followed, keeping his distance so as not to tip off Fratiani that he was being tailed.

Three miles out of Grizzly Pass, Fratiani turned onto a dirt road. T-Rex drove past the road and didn't slow until he'd rounded a curve. As soon as he was reasonably out of sight, he turned around and headed the opposite direction, slowing as he rounded the curve.

As far as he could tell, Fratiani hadn't come out of the dirt road. His Jeep was nowhere in sight.

T-Rex pulled off the road onto another dirt road on the opposite side and drove far enough down it to hide his truck. Then he shifted into Park, leaped out and ran back to the edge of the road, hiding behind the brush, careful not to expose himself.

Nothing moved. After several minutes of close study, T-Rex crossed the road and entered the undergrowth paralleling the dirt road.

Moving in the shadows, he followed the road to a small clearing where Fratiani's Jeep was parked. Another vehicle was backed into the brush. All he could make out of it was the front grille of what appeared to be a pickup.

Fratiani stood beside his Jeep talking to a man who wore a jacket with a hood pulled up around his face.

From where T-Rex stood twenty yards away, he couldn't see the face of the man talking with Fratiani. Nor could he hear what they were saying.

Then Fratiani passed the man an envelope, said

something in more strident tones and climbed back in his Jeep.

To avoid being spotted, T-Rex dropped low behind a tree and waited for the Jeep to pass before he dared glance around the tree. The man Fratiani had been talking with had disappeared, but the vehicle in the trees pulled out. It had a smashed right fender.

T-Rex recognized the truck as the one Clay Ellis had driven the previous day when he'd accosted Sierra at the community center.

What was Ellis doing talking to a land broker on a deserted road in the hills of Wyoming?

Ellis drove away, bumping past him on the rutted road.

As soon as Ellis was out of sight, T-Rex hurried back the way he'd come, using the road. Once he reached the highway, he paused long enough for Ellis's vehicle to disappear out of sight. Then he hurried across the highway, climbed into his truck and followed Ellis into Grizzly Pass.

When he came within cell tower range, he placed a call to Hack. "Check out Clay Ellis's bank accounts. I just saw him have a secret rendezvous with Leo Fratiani on a deserted road three miles outside of Grizzly Pass."

"On it," Hack said. "Where are you now?"

"Back in Grizzly Pass."

"Got word from Major Bailey he'll land in twenty minutes at the fairgrounds."

"That's sooner than expected," T-Rex said. "Did you notify Garner?"

"Couldn't get him. He's probably out of cell phone range by now. Garner didn't expect the pilot to get here at this time. He got away earlier than he thought he would. Will you be able to meet him at the fairgrounds when he lands?"

"I will," T-Rex affirmed. "In the meantime, I'm following Ellis."

"Right. I'll notify Garner when he gets back in cell phone range of the change of plans with Bailey."

"Until I hear differently, I'll go up with Bailey," T-Rex said. He caught sight of Ellis's truck at the far end of Main Street.

Ellis turned at the road leading to the community center.

Great.

Sierra didn't need Ellis disturbing her when she was around the children. Hell, she didn't need the man disturbing her at all.

T-Rex couldn't leave with the helicopter pilot when Sierra might be in danger, especially when her ex-husband could be up to his earlobes in nefarious dealings with a broker from California. Hurrying toward the community center, T-Rex formed a plan. He placed a call to the Mother's Day Out office.

Brenda Larson answered. "Grizzly Pass Mother's Day Out, how may I help you?"

"Miss Larson, this is Rex Trainor. We met yesterday evening."

"I remember. You're the big, tough-looking guy who scared off Sierra's low-life ex."

"Right. I need your assistance."

ONCE AGAIN, SIERRA was outside on the playground with the toddlers when Clay pulled into the parking lot. As quickly as she could, she gathered the children and herded them toward the community center before they saw Clay with all of his bad attitude and demands. She didn't need to traumatize the little ones two days straight. If Clay continued to harass her, she'd have to quit her job with the children. She couldn't risk one of them getting hurt physically or emotionally by Clay's bad temper.

Sierra had begun to wonder if she'd have to move out of Grizzly Pass to get away from Clay. She had friends here, but no family left. She had more reason to leave than stay. She didn't know what was keeping her in the small town where job opportunities were almost nonexistent.

She almost had the children to the door when Clay stepped out of his truck and shouted, "We're not through, you know."

Sierra didn't respond. Instead, she placed a hand

on the child at the rear of the line and urged him forward. "Everyone inside for snack time."

"You shouldn't have hit me with the stun gun," Clay called out. He pulled a metal bar out of the back of his truck and slapped it into his palm.

Sierra's pulse raced. She could visualize it now. Having protected herself using the stun gun had done like she'd said it would. It had only made him madder and more determined to have his way. To top that off, he'd want retribution for the pain and humiliation. He'd take it out on her. If he got close enough to hit her with that bar.

Sierra had no intention of letting him ever lay another finger or anything else on her. But her stun gun was in her purse, hanging on a hook out of reach of little hands, inside the office. And she'd have to get up close to him in order to use it on him. "Get inside, now," she said to the children, her voice brooking no argument.

The toddlers all looked toward the man advancing on them. Some of them cried out, others dashed for the door and tried without any luck to pull on the handle.

Sierra pushed her way through them and grabbed the door handle.

Clay was halfway across the yard before another truck pulled into the parking lot, hopped over the curb and came to a skidding halt in front of Clay, almost hitting the man.

Her heart pounding, Sierra could have cheered when T-Rex dropped down out of the truck.

"Ellis, you're breaking the law," T-Rex said in a cool, even tone.

"The only thing I'll be breaking is you." Clay spun and went after T-Rex.

"Watch out!" Sierra yelled. "He has a steel pipe."

"Get the kids inside." T-Rex waved her toward the building. "I've got this."

Torn between helping T-Rex, who was no match against Clay armed with the pipe, Sierra had no choice but to get the children inside. She jerked open the door and ordered, "Go!"

Most of the toddlers ran inside, but a few clustered around her legs and kept her from moving forward. Eloisa sobbed, her arms wrapped tightly around Sierra's right leg. Marcus, a two-year-old boy, had a hold of the other leg, and a third child stood in front of her, blocking her path, bawling at the top of his lungs.

"Sweet heaven!" Sierra lifted Eloisa into her arms and grabbed Marcus's hand.

Brenda appeared just in time and snatched up the little one blocking the door. "Bring them into the gym."

Sierra followed Brenda inside. Once she had the

toddlers in the gymnasium, she let go of Marcus's hand and peeled Eloisa's arms from around her neck.

"I'll take her." Brenda snatched the redheaded child from Sierra.

"I have to go back out and see what I can do to help."

"I called the sheriff. They are sending a unit."

Sierra didn't wait to respond to her coworker. She ran back out into the yard.

Clay and T-Rex were circling each other.

As soon as Sierra stepped through the door, Clay lunged for T-Rex.

Sierra smothered a scream and stood transfixed as T-Rex caught Clay's wrist and directed it downward, away from his body. The pipe hit the ground hard without harming T-Rex.

T-Rex gave the man a shove from behind, sending him stumbling forward. He righted himself, spun and swung again.

Ducking, T-Rex barely missed being hit in the head.

Clay had swung with so much force, when he whiffed air, he turned all the way around.

T-Rex planted a boot in the man's backside and shoved hard.

Clay went down, thrust the steel pipe out of his way as he fell and landed on his hands and knees. He scrambled to his feet and would have grabbed the pipe, but T-Rex beat him to it, kicking it well out of Clay's reach.

"You need to leave," T-Rex said.

Clay snarled and brushed the dirt from his hands. "I'll leave when Sierra comes with me."

"She's not going anywhere with you," T-Rex said. "She's with me now."

Sierra shook her head. "I don't want anyone hurt. Maybe I should go with him." She crossed the yard to where the two men stood.

"Now you're thinking," Clay said. "Come with me and no one else will get hurt."

"You mean, *you* won't get hurt." T-Rex slipped an arm around Sierra's waist. "She's not with you anymore. Leave her alone."

"She's mine until I tell her she's not anymore."

"Get over yourself, Ellis," T-Rex said, his voice low and threatening. "She doesn't love you."

"Sierra?" Clay stared at her through narrowed eyes.

"I don't think I ever loved you." Sierra swallowed hard and squared her shoulders, remembering every bit of the abuse she'd taken from the man who'd promised to love, honor and cherish her. The man had killed all of her illusions about what a marriage should be. "The first time you hit me, I knew I could never love you, Clay. Leave me alone."

Clay turned his glare on T-Rex. "You did this.

She wouldn't have turned against me if you hadn't gotten in the way."

"I divorced you months ago," Sierra said. "Before Mr. Trainor was even in the picture."

T-Rex nodded. "Face it, Ellis, it's over. Learn to live with it."

A sheriff's vehicle pulled into the drive.

Clay shot one last, piercing glare at T-Rex. "It's not over until I say it's over." Then he climbed into his truck and drove past the sheriff's SUV without stopping or slowing down.

One of the sheriff's deputies got out. "Everything all right here?"

"It is now," Sierra said, leaning into the warmth and strength of T-Rex.

"Want me to go after Ellis?" the deputy asked.

T-Rex glanced down at Sierra, his brow raised.

Sierra nodded. "He needs to learn he can't treat me this way."

The deputy nodded. "I'll let the sheriff know. And let me know if I can help. I'm only a 911 call away." With that parting comment, he turned his vehicle around and left.

Sierra looked up into T-Rex's eyes. "Thank you for being here."

"My pleasure," he said, without removing his arm from around her.

She didn't want to move out of his embrace, but

she had a job to do. "I guess I'd better get back to the children."

"I have an alternative proposal," T-Rex said.

Sierra's heart leaped. "A what?"

"An alternative to going back to work. I need someone to help me with a project I'm working on, but it requires that you come with me right now." He stared at her, his gaze unblinking, almost as if he were willing her to say yes.

When T-Rex looked at her with that level of intensity in his eyes, Sierra found him very hard to resist. "I can't leave," she said. "I'm working."

"No worries," Brenda called out from the doorway, still carrying Eloisa. "Take the rest of the day off. The babies are all down for a nap, and the toddlers are happy playing. I can handle them. Besides, there aren't that many of them, it being Friday and all."

"Are you sure?" Sierra frowned. "I can't leave you to handle all of them."

"I did it before we hired you. I can do it again." Brenda winked. "How many chances do you get to have a hunky man ask you to help him?" Brenda leaned forward and whispered in her ear, "If you don't take him up on it, I'll take your place."

A little stab of jealousy hit Sierra in the gut. She glanced toward T-Rex, a thrill of anticipation making her shiver from top to toe.

"You know you want to," Brenda whispered. "Besides, if you stay here, Clay may come back." She glanced at the children, just beginning to calm down after the second confrontation in as many days they'd had to witness.

A heavy weight of guilt settled in the pit of Sierra's gut. "I can't let this happen to the kids."

Brenda bit her bottom lip. "You didn't let it happen. Clay is responsible."

"Yes, but if I wasn't his ex, he wouldn't be coming to the community center, frightening the babies." Sierra shook her head. "I'm sorry, but I'm going to have to quit until he settles down."

Brenda grabbed her arm. "No. You can't quit on me. The children love you."

"Yes, but I can't risk it. Clay might get more violent and hurt one of them. It's bad enough he's scaring them. The parents aren't going to put up with it for long. Heck, they're already telling me their children are having nightmares." Sierra straightened her shoulders. "No. I have to do this. I thought I could stay in Grizzly Pass, but I'm beginning to see it's just not going to work. Clay will never leave me alone."

Brenda frowned. "Why is he bothering you now? It's been months since your divorce. You'd think he would be over it and moving on."

"Sierra." T-Rex stepped up to the two women. "I

have to go. Will you come with me? Or are you staying here?" He held out his hand.

Sierra stared at his hand as if it would lead her into an alternate universe, a place she'd never considered. Despite the fear of the unknown, she reached out her hand and took his. "I guess I'm going with you."

Brenda tightened her hold on her arm. "Just remember, you're loved and wanted back here. But if you find something better, I'll understand. Oh, and you can't get out of our tour tomorrow. I need you when we take the moms and kiddos to Yellowstone for our ranger-led activity."

Sierra hugged her friend. "Don't worry. I'll be here, bright and early."

Brenda's gaze shifted to T-Rex, and she smiled. "Take care of my friend."

T-Rex nodded. "I will." He tightened his hold on her hand and led her out of the community center. "What was that all about?"

Sierra sighed. "I can't work there anymore."

"Did she fire you?"

"No. I quit. As long as Clay continues to harass me, I can't be around the children." She glanced back at the community center. "I'll miss them."

"You should have had the deputy take him in."

"He'd just be out in a few days and even more annoying. He might harm one of those babies. I know if they were my children I wouldn't want me to be their caregiver. Not as long as Clay keeps coming around."

T-Rex nodded. "I get it."

"Even though we're divorced, he's still managing to run my life."

As the handsome marine held the door for her, Sierra climbed into his truck.

He rounded the vehicle and slid in behind the steering wheel.

"Enough of my troubles." Sierra forced a smile to her face. "What is it I'm going to help you with?"

"I need another pair of eyes."

"Another pair of eyes?"

"I'm going up in a helicopter looking for anything out of the ordinary in the hills."

She leaned forward, her heartbeat skittering against her ribs. "We're going up in a helicopter? I've never been in a helicopter."

"Then this will be a first for you. Are you up for the task?" He started the engine but waited for her response.

"Yes!" She laughed out loud, her entire body shaking with excitement. "When?"

He glanced at his watch. "In five minutes, if I can get to the fairgrounds by then."

Chapter Nine

While they'd waited for clearance for a civilian to go along for the ride in the UH-60 Black Hawk helicopter, T-Rex and the pilot, Major Bailey, and copilot, Lieutenant Strohm, studied several contour maps and the route of the oil pipeline. Some of the larger abandoned gold-rush-era mines were noted on the map, their locations clearly marked.

T-Rex waited, on edge, praying Major Bailey's commander would allow Sierra to join the search. He'd told the major she was part of Homeland Security's platform in Grizzly Pass. It wasn't exactly the truth, but T-Rex wouldn't have gone without Sierra. Not when Ellis would likely stalk her and possibly force her to go with him and hold her hostage who knew where and for how long.

Ellis needed someone to take him out behind a barn and beat some sense into him. Even then, T-Rex doubted the man would listen.

When the approval came through, T-Rex released

the breath he'd been holding. He realized he'd be a whole lot more effective knowing Sierra was right beside him and not at the mercy of her abusive ex-husband.

Once off the ground, T-Rex stopped thinking about Ellis long enough to look out the side of the aircraft.

Major Bailey and his copilot were using the time in the chopper to log flight and training time. By flying through the hills, they'd get some much-needed nap-of-the-earth flying in. At the same time, they'd be flying close enough to the ground that T-Rex and Sierra could look for any signs of extensive road use, vehicles out on old logging or mining trails or people back in the hills where there normally wouldn't be any, especially when not in hunting season.

Sierra sat in the seat beside him, her eyes wide and bright, her hands gripping the safety harness strapped around her lap and shoulders. She looked at once terrified and excited.

T-Rex smiled. The woman might have been in an abusive situation, but she had a lot of gumption and a sense of adventure. She'd do all right once she got far enough from Ellis's influence.

What bothered T-Rex most was the fact he wouldn't be there to run interference against her ex-husband. He'd be out of Grizzly Pass just as soon as they fixed what was wrong in the area.

He leaned toward the open doorway and stared down as the helicopter neared the hills. Based on the map T-Rex had brought along with him depicting the route of the oil pipeline, they were getting close to one of the first points the pipeline inspectors would have checked. It was on the edge of the Beartooth Mountains in a grassy meadow. Nothing appeared out of the ordinary. The dirt road leading up to it was slightly overgrown with grass and bramble.

Flying a direct path, they entered a valley between two hills. The helicopter pilot followed the pipeline to the area where a pipeline inspector had been shot and killed since the military team had arrived in Grizzly Pass. Hovering between the hills, the pilot lowered the aircraft to fifteen feet above the valley floor.

The ground around the pipeline appeared somewhat disturbed. The rotor wash kicked up loose dirt, whipping it around, making it hard to see what was below.

T-Rex didn't know what he expected to find, but the area had seen one death and an attempt by someone to plant dynamite at the same point. Those facts alone gave them good reason to check it out again, despite the full investigation the state crime lab had conducted.

Nothing looked out of the ordinary on the ground

so T-Rex redirected his attention to the hillsides rising up on either side of the valley.

"Anything?" he said into his headset.

"Nothing here," the pilot responded.

"Nothing," the copilot affirmed.

"I'm not sure what I'm looking for, but I don't
see anything moving, or anything that appears out
of place," Sierra said.

"Let's move on toward the border of the Stone
Oak Ranch and the National Park," the pilot said.

T-Rex nodded. "Roger."

The pilot guided the aircraft upward and over the
tops of several ridges.

From his bird's-eye view, T-Rex could see into
the valleys. The aircraft moved slowly, giving them
plenty of time to scour the hillsides looking for caves,
mine shafts and roads leading into and out of the
hills.

As they neared the hills near Stone Oak Ranch
where Olivia Dawson's father had been murdered
by Don Sweeney, T-Rex could see a lot more shadows against the sides of the hills, indicating over-
hangs and caves.

T-Rex leaned against his harness, trying to look
out over the skids of the chopper. "Can you get closer
to the caves?"

In response, Major Bailey tipped the helicopter

and angled it nearer the caves, where he hovered in between two ridges.

"What's that?" Sierra said. "Are those vehicles?"

T-Rex leaned toward her and followed her arm to where she pointed at the side of the hills.

A truck was backed up to a cave. A shadow detached from the darkness of the cave, and a man dressed in camouflage stared up at the helicopter. He looked back to the cave and appeared to be shouting, not that they could hear him over the roar of the rotors.

A moment later, another man joined him, carrying a short tube. He extended it to double its length, settled it on his shoulder and aimed it at the helicopter.

"Rocket launcher! Get out of here!" T-Rex cried.

The pilot pulled back on the controls and goosed the throttle, sending them climbing higher, out of the valley.

"Brace yourself!" T-Rex reached over, grabbed Sierra's hand and squeezed it.

Something slammed into the back of the helicopter, sending it spinning around to the right.

"We're hit," the copilot shouted into the headset.

The pilot struggled with the controls, steadied the craft and pulled the nose upward as it rushed toward the side of a cliff.

T-Rex couldn't look away from the bare rock cliff

they were rushing toward, as if he was mesmerized by his forthcoming death.

At the last moment, the chopper lifted up, skimming over the top of the ridge, the skids scraping against the hard surface.

Major Bailey looked around. "We have to find a place to put this baby down."

T-Rex looked around at the rugged terrain.

"It needs to be wide enough to allow for a sloppy landing."

"South. Go south toward Stone Oak Ranch."

"Those men who shot at us are moving," Sierra said, leaning toward the open door. "They're on ATVs."

"They're following us," the copilot confirmed.

"Can you get us farther away before you land?" T-Rex asked.

The craft shuddered and dipped. Major Bailey held on to the controls with both hands, his body straining. "We'll be lucky to land in one piece."

"Over there. On that knoll." The copilot pointed to a barren hilltop with a fence stretching across one side and angling downward into a valley.

"That's on Stone Oak Ranch," T-Rex said. "We could get help from the owner, Olivia Dawson.

"It will take at least an hour to hike down to her," T-Rex said. "It took thirty minutes to get to that point on four-wheelers from her ranch house."

"Those men on the ATVs might catch up to us." Sierra twisted in her seat, staring at the ground below.

As the pilot concentrated on flying the Black Hawk to the open knoll, the copilot put out a mayday call.

Twenty yards from the projected landing zone, the chopper sputtered, the rotor slowed and the descent came quicker than expected.

"It's going to be a bumpy landing," the pilot said.

T-Rex held tighter to Sierra's hand and gave her a tight smile. "We've got this."

No sooner had he said the words, the helicopter slammed into the ground and skidded across the knoll, coming to a stop near the other end, at the edge of a sheer one-hundred-foot drop.

Everyone remained seated until the rotors stopped moving and the pilot turned off the engine.

Then the pilot unbuckled his harness and turned in his seat to look at each person in the craft. "Everyone all right?"

The copilot nodded.

"I'm okay," T-Rex said.

Sierra grinned. "That was amazing."

Her infectious smile made T-Rex smile, as well. "Good job, Major Bailey."

"Thanks, but it would be even better if we hadn't been hit in the first place." He flung aside his harness and got out of the helicopter, stepping up to the edge of the cliff they'd almost gone over.

T-Rex helped Sierra out of her harness, slid out of his seat and held open his arms for her.

She let him help her out of the craft and onto her feet. Her glance followed the pilot standing a few feet away, looking down. "That was close." Sierra leaned into T-Rex.

He wrapped his arm around her waist and pulled her tightly against him. "Yes, it was." Too close.

The whine of small engines reminded him the men who'd lobbed a rocket at them were on their way through the hills to find them.

"What do you want to bet they will be armed?" the copilot said.

T-Rex nodded. "We need to get moving if we want to stay a reasonable distance ahead."

"I can't leave the aircraft here." Major Bailey backed away from the cliff's edge and joined them. "There's no telling what they'll do to it."

"The army can afford to lose a chopper. They can't afford to lose a trained pilot," T-Rex said.

The copilot nodded. "He's right. Without weapons to defend ourselves, we'd be sitting ducks."

"Were you able to contact the sheriff?" Sierra asked.

"We put out a mayday call but didn't get a response, so we have no idea if the call was heard."

The copilot slipped his headset back on and sat back in his seat, fiddling with the radio dial on the control panel.

T-Rex glanced at his cell phone. No signal.

A moment later, the copilot got out of the helicopter, tossed his headset onto the seat and shook his head. "The radio is dead."

"Then we're on our own." T-Rex ran toward the other side of the hill and glanced down into a valley. Five men on four-wheelers were racing along a trail, headed their way.

T-Rex turned and almost ran into Sierra. "We have to get out of here." He took her hand and hurried back to the pilot and copilot. "We only have a few minutes before five aggressors top this hill. We need to get down off of here and to somewhere we can take advantage of cover and concealment."

"We don't want them to have the opportunity to shoot at us on the way down, so we'd better hustle." The pilot glanced around. "Are you familiar with the area? Do you know which way to the Dawson woman's ranch house?"

"Follow me." T-Rex led the way down from the hill, taking a trail barely wide enough for a four-wheeler. He'd been up there a couple of days earlier when he and the team had inspected the hill and the area around it, searching for a similar group of five marauders who'd given chase to Hawkeye and Olivia.

They had not been successful at locating the area from which they'd come. Numerous trails wound their way through the hills and mountains, weaving through the silent remains of a once-busy mining community back in the late 1800s. They'd spent a couple of days taking different trails, but they hadn't been able to find the men.

If they didn't get down to an area that provided cover and concealment soon, the attackers on four-wheelers would find them and pick them off, one-by-one. They hadn't hesitated in firing a rocket at a government helicopter, and they wouldn't balk at shooting four people.

They half walked and half ran down the trail, slipping on loose gravel. T-Rex worried Sierra would trip and fall over the edge. He held her hand, refusing to let her tumble to her death. Not on his watch.

As they neared the floor of a narrow valley, T-Rex paused and glanced up at the hill they'd just vacated.

The pilot and copilot had stopped to catch their breath. Each was bent over, hands on their knees. They'd pushed hard to get this far, and it hadn't been easy with the loose gravel and treacherous terrain.

T-Rex could hear the roar of the four-wheeler engines. He spun and grabbed Sierra's hand. She was winded and her cheeks were bright pink, but she gave him a brief smile.

"Are you all right?" T-Rex asked.

She nodded, glancing up at the hill they'd come down. Then she squared her shoulders. "Let's move. They're almost on us."

The engine noise grew louder as T-Rex led them toward a jumble of boulders lying at the base of an enormous overhang. If they could make it there, they'd have concealment and cover. It also might leave them trapped and outnumbered five to four. With no weapons but their minds, they'd have to come up with a plan. Either they would lay low and pray the attackers would give up and move on, or they'd have to fight back, barehanded.

Ten yards from the first boulder big enough to offer any kind of protection, the crack of gunfire echoed off the hillsides.

Dirt shot up next to T-Rex's feet. "Run!" he yelled, pushing Sierra in front of him. She picked up the pace, her feet flying over the rocks and gravel.

Another crack sounded, and the copilot fell to his knees.

"Damn. He got my leg." He tried to get up but fell back to the ground.

Sierra slowed and started to turn back.

"Don't stop. Keep moving," T-Rex ordered.

"But—" She hesitated. A bullet hit the ground beside her.

"Just go!" His pulse racing and unable to block the bullets from hitting Sierra, T-Rex flung the copilot over his shoulder and ran as fast as he could, weighted down by the man.

"Let me help," the pilot offered.

"Help by getting Sierra to a safe place."

The pilot nodded and ran to catch up to Sierra.

More gunfire echoed off the rock walls of the valley.

Sierra reached the boulder first and ducked behind, followed by the pilot. A few steps behind them, T-Rex made it to the boulder and dropped the man on the ground.

"How bad is it?" T-Rex asked.

The copilot gritted his teeth. "I think I can get around, but I might need a little help."

T-Rex nodded to the pilot. "You stand watch. Let me know how close they get."

Major Bailey nodded and eased his head around the opposite side of the boulder for a quick peek, ducking back as gunfire rang out. "They're standing at the top of the hill, their weapons aimed in our direction."

T-Rex pulled his knife from the scabbard strapped to his belt and tore the leg of the copilot's jumpsuit. He handed the fabric to Sierra. "I need long strips."

She quickly ripped the pant leg into four-inch-wide strips, wadded up one into a thick pad and pressed it to the man's wound. As she held the pad, T-Rex made quick work of wrapping the other strip around the copilot's leg. He tied a knot over the pad and helped the man to his feet.

"Think you and Sierra can make your way to the back of this stand of rocks?"

The copilot nodded.

Sierra draped the man's arm over her shoulder and wrapped one of hers around his waist. "We'll manage. But what about you two?"

"They're coming down," the major said.

"That gives us seconds to take positions and get ready to do what we can to protect ourselves." T-Rex shot a glance at Sierra. "Your job is to get Lieutenant Strohm as far back as possible and hide behind some really big rocks. If this turns into a shooting match, I don't want you two catching stray bullets."

She didn't move, her lips thinning into a straight line. "But what about you?"

"I can take care of myself." He nodded toward Major Bailey. "And I have backup."

Her brows dipped. "And no weapons."

"Can't help that," he said. "But you're wasting valuable time and putting the lieutenant in danger. Move!"

She jumped and started weaving through the huge boulders that had fallen from the side of the cliff, helping the copilot along as best she could.

Once Sierra was out of sight, T-Rex shot a glance

at the major. "Sir, are you ready to play a game of cat and mouse?"

The pilot pulled a knife from the strap around his calf and nodded. "Let's do this."

T-Rex melted back behind the surrounding boulders and hunkered low. He circled back toward the trail where the riders were coming from and waited. They arrived in a swift procession, slowing as they reached the maze of boulders. Each man wore a black helmet and carried his rifle either resting in a plastic gun boot attached to the ATV or slung over his shoulder within easy reach.

After four of the five riders passed by him, T-Rex made his move. The last four-wheeler came abreast of where T-Rex was hiding. T-Rex leaped out, grabbed the man from the back of the ATV and dragged him behind the boulder, his neck in a headlock. Without the man on the vehicle, the ATV rolled to a standstill.

While the others were just coming to a halt, firing their weapons into the air, T-Rex tightened his hold around the man's neck, cutting off his air until he passed out.

T-Rex pulled the AR-15 rifle from over the man's shoulder and dragged the attacker's shirt off and down his arms, quickly twisting it into a knot around his wrists behind his back. It might not hold him long, but it had to be enough for the moment.

T-Rex grabbed the rifle and checked the thirty-round magazine. Then he eased up to the side of one of the boulders and opened fire, shooting at the ground near their tires, not giving them a chance to dismount.

The riders yelped, hit their throttles and raced around a bend in the trail and out of sight.

"Major, we have maybe a minute before they return on foot," T-Rex called out.

The major hurried toward him. "How the heck did you get that?"

"I borrowed it from the young man on the ground over there." He pointed to the man he'd jumped.

The attacker was starting to wake up. Still wearing the black helmet, he shook his head and cursed, struggling to free himself from the bonds of his shirt.

"The others will be back," T-Rex said, "but will probably sneak in. We need to make sure they don't get to Sierra and Strohm."

"There are only the two of us. How are we going to keep four men at bay?" Bailey asked.

"We have to keep our eyes open and be smarter than they are." T-Rex led the way through the boulders to the far end past which the riders had driven in their hurry to get away from the flying bullets.

T-Rex handed the AR-15 to the pilot and positioned him behind a large cluster of boulders. "If they come your way, don't wait for them to shoot before pulling the trigger. I guarantee they won't be as nice to you."

The major nodded and crawled down in between the rocks. "What about you?"

"I'll find them before they find me." He held his knife in his hand and slipped in between the standing boulders, working his way through them to the point at which he anticipated the four men to breach the rugged array of rocks and giant fallen portions of the cliff. He paused, watching the trails leading back to him and the slope of the hillside.

The sun had made progress toward the jagged edges of the ridgelines towering on either side of the narrow valley. Before long it would be dark. The riders could be waiting for dusk to make their moves. Or not. At dusk, they would all be at a disadvantage.

T-Rex stood ready, straining his ears for even the slightest of sounds.

Chapter Ten

Sierra half walked, half carried Lieutenant Strohm deeper into the jumble of giant boulders, picking her way over the smaller rocks and around the larger ones. The sound of ATV engines moved closer until they had to be on the trail where she'd left T-Rex and Major Bailey. She moved as fast as she could to get Strohm out of harm's way.

Finally, the injured man ground to a halt. Leaning heavily on her, he whispered, "I can't…keep going."

Her back aching from the strain, Sierra looked around, searching for a place to hide and praying their attackers wouldn't see her or the lieutenant before they found one. "You can't stop out in the open. We need to get you hidden."

He agreed. Between the two of them, they got him wedged behind a pile of big rocks, completely out of sight to anyone passing by.

Moments later, gunfire echoed off the rock walls, and Sierra ducked low next to Strohm. Her heart pounded hard against her ribs as she knelt behind the boulders, wondering whether T-Rex and the major had been hit.

Then she heard the sound of engines moving away. Once the noise had faded, she counted to ten and slowly straightened.

The lieutenant grabbed for her. "What are you doing?"

"I have to see if they were hit. They could be injured and need help." She peeled the lieutenant's hand from her arm. "Will you be all right?"

"I'll be fine, but I'm worried about you," he said. "Your marine would kick my butt if I let anything happen to you."

He wasn't her marine, and the copilot was in no shape to protect her, but now wasn't the time for Sierra to correct him. She had to find T-Rex.

Easing her way back toward the trail, she pushed to the north, hoping to swing around and come from behind where she'd heard the ATVs stop. She grabbed a rock the size of her hand. It wasn't much of a weapon, but it was all she had in case someone attacked her or T-Rex.

As she neared the trail, she hid behind a boulder and studied the path beyond. It was empty. No one stood nearby or lay on the ground.

Then she heard someone grunting, the sound of gravel being disturbed and muttered curses.

Sierra eased back behind the larger boulders and followed the noise.

She had almost reached the source of the sound when she noticed a black helmet on the ground and a torn shirt. As she stepped toward them, she caught a flash of movement out of the corner of her eye. Before she had time to move or scream, a hand clamped over her mouth and an arm wrapped around her belly, trapping one of her arms to her side.

Heart pounding, she tried to remain calm. Whoever had her was bare-armed and smelled of smoke and body odor.

"You're coming with me," he whispered.

The hell she was. She flung her free hand with the rock up behind her, crashing it into the man's head.

He cursed, and for a brief moment, his hold on her loosened.

Sierra broke free, spun and kneed him in the groin.

He went down, his face turning a sick shade of green.

Her adrenaline still firing through her veins, she kicked him in the chin, sending him flying backward to land on the ground.

Sierra stood with her rock in her hand, breathing hard, ready for anything the punk might try next.

When he didn't move, she inched toward him.

The man was out cold.

Quickly, before he came to, she grabbed the abandoned shirt, ripped it into strips, rolled him over and tied his wrists securely. Then she tied his ankles. The jerk wasn't going to come after her or anyone else in her party, if she could help it. Wadding up the last piece of fabric, she stuffed it into his mouth.

Armed with her rock, she slipped back among the boulders, determined to find T-Rex and the pilot. What had happened to them?

It would be night soon, which would make it even more difficult to find them if they were injured.

She glanced up at the rocky hillside ahead of her and noticed a shadowy figure slipping down between the trees and rocks.

Was it another member of the gang of ATV riders who'd attacked their helicopter? She stood still, watching as the man made it to the edge of the boulder field carrying what appeared to be a military-grade rifle.

Where were T-Rex and the pilot?

The sun ducked behind the hills above them, casting the landscape into a deep, gray shadow. With adrenaline wearing off and no sun to warm the air around her, Sierra shivered.

Another shadowy figure followed the first, edging his way down the slope. Then another. That was three, plus the one she'd tied up made four. Where was number five?

Sierra stayed put, afraid to move and draw attention to herself. She had yet to locate T-Rex. Most likely he was hiding among the boulders, waiting for his chance to take down the attackers, one at a time. He wasn't injured or dead. Sierra refused to believe the combat veteran would have exposed himself to the gunfire.

Straining to hear footsteps or voices, she pressed herself back into a crevice and waited.

T-REX HEARD SOUNDS from both in front of him and to the rear of where he stood. He was only mildly reassured by the fact that the man he'd knocked out behind him was unarmed. The men scurrying down the hill toward him still carried their AR-15s. He almost wished he hadn't given the major the rifle. If he had it now, he could have picked off the attackers as they worked their way down the slope.

Armed with only a knife, T-Rex's four-to-one odds were pretty lousy. He moved silently through the boulder field, easing from shadow to shadow until he was close to where the men would enter the rock-strewn area. His best chance was to get them one at a time. That plan would work only if the ATV riders split up.

He waited as the first man entered the field several yards away from him.

T-Rex backtracked and circled a huge boulder,

praying he'd correctly anticipated the man's path. With his knife in hand, he listened.

The rattle of gravel alerted him to his quarry on the other side of the boulder. When the man in black stepped into view, he didn't see what hit him.

Neither did T-Rex.

He hadn't even touched the man, when he heard a loud thud and the guy dropped to the ground with a grunt and lay still.

Stunned, T-Rex glanced up to find Sierra standing with a big rock in her hand, her eyes wide, her breathing coming in ragged gasps.

T-Rex must have moved because Sierra's gaze shot from the man on the ground to him. She stifled a squeal and backed up several steps before she realized it was him.

A soft curse and the shuffle of gravel warned T-Rex others were coming. He shoved Sierra behind him. Then he took the man's arms and dragged him backward, hiding him among the rocks. He removed a knife from the man's belt and took his rifle.

The crack of gunfire filled the air nearby.

T-Rex grabbed Sierra and rolled her to the ground, throwing his body over hers. The shooting continued in spurts, very near to where they lay hidden behind the boulder.

At one pause in the firing, he thought he heard the sound of engines in the distance.

More shots rang out, and then another pause ensued. A deep voice shouted, "Vehicles coming! Get out! Now!"

The man Sierra had knocked out stirred, sat up and looked around.

"Move! Move! Move!" the same guy shouted, and more shots were fired in rapid succession from the semiautomatic weapons.

T-Rex pointed his weapon at the man sitting up and touched a finger to his lips.

The man took one look at T-Rex, rolled to his side and scurried behind a big rock.

"Don't let him get away!" Sierra urged, in a quiet, yet insistent voice.

"I'm not leaving you," T-Rex whispered.

"Then shoot him," she said.

"If I do, I'll give away our position."

"But he's getting away." She struggled beneath him.

T-Rex refused to let her up. "I'd rather he got away than you get killed."

When she tried again to get up, he touched a finger to her lips. "Shh."

She went still, her eyes wide, her chest rising and falling beneath his.

Heat filled him and raced to his groin. Sierra's soft curves beneath him and the adrenaline of the chase rushing through his blood had him hard in seconds.

But now was not the time to have sensual thoughts about the woman he covered with his body.

The sound of feet moving through gravel came to them from so close, it had to be on the other side of the boulder.

T-Rex quietly rolled off Sierra and sat up with the AR-15 rifle in his hands. If the attackers found them, T-Rex would empty the magazine, protecting Sierra.

Major Bailey tiptoed into the gap between the rocks, the rifle T-Rex had given him nestled against his shoulder, his hand on the trigger. He turned, aiming the weapon at T-Rex.

T-Rex held up his free hand and whispered, "Don't shoot."

The man's shoulders relaxed. "Oh, thank God. For a moment, I thought you were one of them." He jerked his head toward the trail. "There are more ATVs coming up the trail from the south. The guys who were shooting at us scattered into the hills."

T-Rex climbed to his feet, reached down to give Sierra a hand up and pulled her into the crook of his arm. "We need to be ready in case they aren't any friendlier than the others."

The major glanced at Sierra. "Where's Strohm?"

"I have him tucked away pretty nicely. But I better find him before it gets too dark to see." She started to step away from T-Rex.

He didn't let go of his hold around her. "We'll

find him when we know for sure the ATV riders are gone and the new ones headed this way aren't here to harm us."

Sierra nodded.

The three of them eased up to the edge of the trail.

T-Rex insisted Sierra stay farther behind. He and the major aimed their weapons at the approaching vehicles.

Four ATVs rolled into sight.

T-Rex waited until he recognized the jacket of the man in front of the pack. It was the same jacket, with the Department of Homeland security emblem on it, Kevin Garner had worn that morning.

T-Rex lowered his weapon, raised a hand and stepped out of the shadows.

Garner leaped down from his four-wheeler and pulled off his helmet. "Holy hell, T-Rex. What happened?"

T-Rex glanced at the hillside where their attackers had run to. "You might want to step into the shadows. Up until a few minutes ago, we were under fire."

Garner's brows rose, and he joined T-Rex, the major and Sierra near the stand of boulders. He waved to the others, who all dismounted and joined them, removing their helmets.

Hawkeye, Ghost and Caveman crowded close.

"We got the mayday from the sheriff's office that

your aircraft had been hit and was crash-landing in the hills," Garner said.

"Dude, you had us all worried," Hawkeye said.

"*You* were worried?" T-Rex chuckled. "You should have been on the helicopter." He clapped a hand on Major Bailey's shoulders. "This man did an incredible job landing the chopper." He shoved his AR-15 at Ghost. "But right now, we have an injured copilot we need to get to medical attention. Can you cover us?"

Ghost hefted the weapon in his hands, released the magazine, inspected it and slipped it back in. "Gotcha covered."

T-Rex turned to Sierra. "Think you can find him?"

HER HEART STILL racing and her body on fire from the pressure of T-Rex's pressed against it earlier, Sierra nodded and took off through the maze. She stopped a couple of times and studied the paths. Everything looked a bit different in the dusky light, but she recognized the landscape and moved on. Finally, she came to what would appear to the others to be nothing more than a pile of big rocks.

Sierra ducked between them and found the copilot, lying on the ground. "Hey, Lieutenant, I told you I'd be back."

"I swear you're an angel," he said, his voice

strained, the pain making his mouth tight. His face was pale, and he struggled to stand.

"We could use a hand," Sierra called out, moving quickly to slip her arm around the man.

T-Rex stepped into the gap and looped one of the lieutenant's arms over his shoulder.

"Let me." Caveman entered the hiding place and motioned for Sierra to move out so that he could get in and take Strohm's other side. They eased him out into the open.

Forming a two-man fireman's carry, T-Rex and Caveman transported the copilot to the trail.

After they settled the lieutenant on the ground, T-Rex straightened. "If he hasn't gotten away, we caught one of the guys who was with those who shot us down." He started toward the stand of rocks to the north end of the trail.

Sierra joined him. "He's not where he was before."

"No?" T-Rex frowned.

She shook her head. "But he's not far."

T-Rex's frown deepened. "And you know this because?"

She shrugged and gave him a twisted grin. "I have a mean arm when it comes to rocks."

"I've seen that arm in action." He chuckled. "It was pretty impressive."

They found the man where Sierra had left him bound and gagged.

"Are you sure you weren't a secret agent in a past life?" Garner asked.

She shook her head. "No, but I watch enough movies and television to know how to incapacitate the bad guy."

They pulled the gag from the man's mouth and dragged him out to the trail.

Now that she had time to study him, Sierra thought she recognized him. "Cody Rausch?"

The young man glared at her but refused to speak.

She shook her head and planted her hands on her hips. "What will your father say when he finds out you've been shooting down government helicopters?"

He still didn't say anything, just continued to glare at Sierra.

"Fine. But you know the sheriff will be talking with you as soon as we get back to town."

Dusk had settled over the mountains, casting the group into a shadowy darkness.

A few minutes later, a rescue helicopter flew overhead, shining a bright spotlight down on them. The aircraft landed on the hillside above them, and the trained rescue team hurried down with a basket. They radioed back to the chopper to bring another.

Once they had the copilot and the bad guy in baskets, the rescue workers and the Safe Haven team carried the men back up the hill and loaded them into the helicopter. Major Bailey boarded the helicopter with his lieutenant.

Garner stood beside the helicopter to address his team. "I'm going with them to the hospital. I hope to be there when the sheriff interrogates Rausch. This might be the breakthrough we've been looking for. I trust you can get back to Grizzly Pass on your own?"

"We've got this," Ghost said.

Sierra wasn't as confident. Night had settled in. Thankfully, each of the ATVs had headlights, but the trails were treacherous in the daylight. They'd be downright deadly at night.

They waited while the helicopter took off, headed for the closest hospital, then the four men mounted the four-wheelers.

T-Rex tilted his head toward Sierra. "You can ride with me."

"I wasn't planning on riding with anyone else," she said, her words soft enough only T-Rex would hear. She slid on behind him and wrapped her arms around his waist. "I hope you know where you're going, because I don't."

He nodded. "I've been on this trail before. Though it was in the light of day at the time."

"We'll take it slow," Caveman said.

They left the boulder field. Caveman took the lead, T-Rex and Sierra behind him. Hawkeye and Ghost brought up the rear.

The night had turned cold, the temperature dropping close to freezing, even though it wasn't yet fall.

Sierra leaned close to T-Rex, absorbing as much warmth from his body as she could. By the time they reached the Stone Oak ranch house, she was shivering uncontrollably, her toes numb and her entire body exhausted.

Olivia Dawson met them at the gate and ushered them through, closing it behind them. "Come inside. I just happened to make a huge pot of beef stew. You look hungry and cold."

"Sounds like heaven," Sierra said, her teeth chattering. "Hi, Liv. Glad you're back in Grizzly Pass. I missed you." She hugged the rancher, glad to see the woman and the house ahead with the glow of lights welcoming them.

Sierra stumbled, her cold feet barely able to carry her. She refused to give up now. Not when she was so close to a warm fire and food.

T-Rex came up behind her, scooped her into his arms and marched toward the house.

"I can walk," Sierra protested, though she didn't struggle. Being in T-Rex's arms meant she got to rest her body against his warmer one. She leaned her cheek against his chest and tucked her hands between them. "I don't think I've ever been quite that cold."

"We didn't go prepared for the possibilities."

She snorted. "Who would have guessed our helicopter would be shot down? Things like that don't happen in America."

His lips thinned and his brows descended. "Yeah, well, sometimes they do."

Caveman reached the door first and opened it for T-Rex and Sierra.

T-Rex entered and went straight for the living room, where he laid Sierra on a couch by a roaring fire and smothered her in throw blankets.

She laughed. "I think one will do."

"You might have hypothermia," he said. "You need to bring your body temperature back up." T-Rex tucked the edges of the blankets around and beneath her until she couldn't move her arms.

"Seriously. I feel like a mummy." She wiggled until she could get her hands and arms out. "I'm okay. Really." As if to belie her statement, she shivered violently. Her cheeks heated, and she shrugged. "At least I'm on my way to being okay."

When T-Rex dived for the edges of the blankets again, Sierra touched his cheek. "I'm okay." She smiled up into his eyes. "Thank you."

He frowned and stood straight. "I shouldn't have brought you with me today. I got you involved where you shouldn't have been."

"I'm glad you took me. I've never flown in a helicopter."

"And I bet you've never crashed in one either." He

tucked a strand of her hair behind her ear. "I hope like hell you never crash-land in one again."

"We have hot cocoa for anyone who wants some," Liv called out. She entered the living room swinging a sack of puffy white marshmallows. Hawkeye followed carrying a large tray filled with mugs and a pot of steaming cocoa.

After they all had their mugs filled with brew and a marshmallow or two, the men settled in the leather seats scattered around the spacious living room.

T-Rex paced in front of the fireplace, having sipped only once on his cocoa before setting it on the mantel. "That was too close."

"Now that we're all in the same room, tell us about it," Ghost urged.

T-Rex recounted what had taken place, from leaving in the helicopter to spotting the truck backed up to the cave. When he came to the part about being shot down from the sky, he was interrupted.

"They shot you down with a rocket?" Ghost exclaimed. "Holy hell, what kind of arsenal do they have?"

Caveman leaned forward, his hands clasped together. "We need to get back up in those hills first thing in the morning."

"Hell, we need to have people on the roads, watching for any movement out of the hills." Hawkeye rose from his seat and paced the opposite direction of T-Rex. "They might decide to pack it all up and move it to an alternate location tonight."

"I'll coordinate with Garner and the sheriff. Who's up for a night shift?"

T-Rex raised a hand. "I'm out. I'm worried that now that Sierra's involved, she'll be targeted."

Ghost nodded. "I think between us and the sheriff's department, we can handle the night. But we need to be out looking tomorrow." He nodded toward T-Rex. "Except you."

Sierra directed a frown toward T-Rex. "I don't need you to look out for me tomorrow. I'm headed to the park at Yellowstone. I won't be anywhere around."

His brows furrowed as he studied her. "Alone?"

She smiled. "No. I'm going with my coworker, Brenda, and several mothers. We're taking some children to the park since they didn't make it there the day they were kidnapped."

T-Rex's brows dipped deeper. "Are you sure it's a good idea?"

"No one is going to kidnap half a dozen women in a couple of cars headed for the park. It's not like there will be a bus of children with only three adults. We'll be okay." She shook her head. "We can't stay home, afraid to get outside because of some band of troublemakers."

"I'll come with you," T-Rex said.

As much as Sierra loved having him around, she couldn't take him away from his duties. "You have a job. I'm not a part of that. We will be fine on our own, and the vehicles are already full."

"She's right," Hawkeye said. "Besides, we'll need all the help we can get if the hills are full of Free America homegrown terrorists."

For a long moment, T-Rex stared at Sierra. He didn't appear happy about her going off without him. But he didn't have a say in the matter. He'd be out of Grizzly Pass soon, and she'd be back to living alone.

A deep shiver shook her frame. A couple of days ago, she'd been perfectly happy to be alone.

Since she'd met T-Rex, everything had changed.

Chapter Eleven

After the hearty dinner of beef stew Liv provided, Ghost gave T-Rex and Sierra a ride back to Grizzly Pass and dropped them at T-Rex's truck at the fairgrounds. From there, T-Rex drove Sierra back to the bed-and-breakfast.

He used his key to open the front entrance. Low lights were left on in the hallway and the front living space for those guests returning late or wanting to relax in front of the dying embers in the fireplace.

Sierra passed the living area and climbed the stairs slowly, trailing her hand along the banister. She had to be bone tired after the stress of the afternoon. How many women held up so well after surviving a helicopter crash landing, being shot at and attacked by a man intent on killing her?

T-Rex was surprised and proud of how well she'd handled herself. He chuckled every time he remembered the image of her standing over that bad guy with a big rock in her hand. The woman had gumption.

When they reached her room, she paused and turned toward him. "Thanks again for saving me today."

"I think you have that backward. I should be thanking you."

She smiled. "I guess we could call it even."

He cupped her cheek in his hand. "You are an amazing woman."

She leaned into his palm and closed her eyes. "No, I'm an ordinary woman who did what she had to do in the face of adversity."

"You have your opinion, and I have mine." He brushed his thumb across her lips. "And right now, I want to kiss you so badly I can't resist. Tell me no and I'll leave you alone."

Sierra opened her eyes and stared up into his. "I'm not saying no." Her voice came out in a breathy whisper. She laid her hand on his chest and leaned up on her toes, lifting her chin.

T-Rex had no choice but to kiss those full, luscious lips. He couldn't have resisted had he tried.

His mouth crashed down on hers, and he brought his hands to her hips, pulling her close.

She parted her lips and met his tongue as he thrust inside her mouth.

T-Rex had never felt such an intense need to take this woman, to touch every part of her body and bury himself inside her. He caressed her tongue with his, twisting, sliding and loving the lingering taste of hot cocoa.

Her hands slid up his chest and around the back of his neck. Her calf circled his, and she pressed her sex against his thigh.

T-Rex groaned and ran his fingers up her back, buried them in her hair and tugged gently, pulling her head back. Then he left her mouth to trail kisses down the long, smooth line of her throat. Sweet beauty, her skin was so soft.

When he reached the rise of her collarbone, he paused and lifted his head to breathe and slow his pulse. That little pause allowed his brain to catch up and remind him who he was and who she was.

He was a marine, destined to return to his unit and deploy.

Sierra was a beautiful, desirable woman who'd been abused by her ex-husband. She deserved a man who would be there for her every day. A man who would shower her with the tender, loving care she so desperately deserved.

He wasn't that man.

He dropped his hands to his side and stepped away. "I can't do this."

She blinked her eyes open and stared up at him. "Did I do something wrong?"

He shook his head, every instinct telling him to take her into his arms and make sweet love to her through the rest of the night. But his brain couldn't allow it. "I'm not the right guy for you, darlin'. You deserve so much better."

"I don't want better," she said, closing the gap he'd put between them. "I want you." When she raised her hands to touch him, he grabbed them and held them away.

"I can only take so much. If we continue along this path, I won't be able to stop."

She smiled and shook her head. "I don't want you to stop."

"I could be gone tomorrow," he reminded her.

"Either one of us could have been gone today." She inhaled deeply and let it out. "Look, if it makes you feel better, I'm not looking for commitment. It's just that I don't want to spend the night alone. Not after all that happened today. You've been with me all day. Please." She held out her hand. "Don't leave me now."

He stared at her face and then down at her hand, and felt the walls of his resistance crumbling around him.

Finally, he took her hand. "I don't want you to regret what could happen between us tonight."

"I'll regret it more if we don't have this one night together." She lifted his hand to her cheek and gave him a soft, sexy smile that turned his knees to butter. "I need a shower. So do you." She didn't say more, just led him into the shared bathroom and closed the door behind them.

Once inside, she turned the handle on the shower faucet, tested the heat and then faced him. Her cheeks were pink, and she was chewing on her lip.

"I've never seduced a man before." She ran her fingers down the front of his shirt, pushing the buttons loose as she went. "I haven't been on a date since high school."

T-Rex dragged in a shaky breath and let it out. "You must be doing something right because I'm so turned on right now I can barely see straight."

She laughed softly and tugged his shirt loose from his waistband. "Seeing straight isn't a requirement tonight. In fact, it might be a detractor."

When she reached for the button on his jeans, he put his hand over hers, stopping her there.

Sierra glanced up, wide-eyed. "What?"

He squeezed her hands gently. "Wait." He pulled his wallet from his back pocket and extracted two foil packets.

She smiled and shook her head. "I'm clean of any STDs and I can't get pregnant. But you're way ahead of me. I didn't even think about protection."

"For you more than for me. If there's even a chance of getting you pregnant, I wouldn't want to leave you to manage on your own."

She muttered something that sounded like *I'd take my chances*.

"What did you say?" he asked.

"I was married for seven years and never got pregnant. It won't happen now. But I'm all for protection." She reached for his button again, worked it loose and then slid the zipper downward, taking her sweet time.

T-Rex gritted his teeth, ready to rip off his clothes and hers. But he didn't want to frighten her. She'd been through enough with her ex-husband. Being a Neanderthal now would only reinforce all men were like Ellis. And he was nothing like her ex-husband. He cared enough about the women he had sex with to see to their satisfaction before his own.

But Sierra was testing his ability to hold back. When her knuckles brushed across his erection, he nearly came unglued. He captured her wrists in his and raised them above her head. Then he reached for the hem of her shirt, dragged it up over her head and tossed it on the counter.

She wore a lacy pink bra that framed her breasts beautifully. Unfortunately, it had to go in order for him to access the nipples beneath, puckering into tight little peaks.

Reaching behind her, he fumbled with the hooks. And fumbled some more. He couldn't seem to get the hooks to release. "I'm sorry. I'm way out of practice."

She laughed, tucked her arm up behind her back

and slipped the hooks free. But she didn't remove the garment. Instead she cocked her brow.

T-Rex took it from there and slipped the straps from her arm, freeing her breasts. They spilled out and bounced a little in the process.

T-Rex cupped the rounded orbs in his palms and lifted as if weighing them. "Beautiful."

Sierra pressed her hands to the backs of his and inhaled, pushing deeper into his hold. "If we don't hurry, the water will get cold before we get in."

In seconds they were both naked and in the shower, laughing.

"Shh." Sierra pressed a finger to T-Rex's lips. He promptly sucked it into his mouth and bit down gently before releasing it.

"We can't have our landlady coming up to check on all the commotion," he said.

"No." Sierra leaned up on her toes and pressed her lips to his. "We can't," she said into his mouth.

T-Rex's laughter ended and his hunger built. He drew her body against his and stepped under the shower's spray, letting it run over them both.

Sierra squirted body wash liquid into her hand and ran it over his shoulders and across his chest, rubbing until lather built and ran down his torso.

He returned the gesture, running his hands over the swells of her breasts, down to her narrow waist and across the flare of her hips. Then he bent to kiss one of her nipples, rolling the tip between his teeth.

Her back arched, pressing more of her into his mouth. He took it, sucking her breast, flicking the tip with his tongue until she moaned and dug her fingers into his hair and held him even closer.

When he'd had his fill of one side, he switched his attention to the other.

Sierra moaned and ran her leg up the back of his, rubbing her sex against his thigh.

"What did I do with those packets?" he asked, his voice as tight as his body.

She fished one out of the soap dish, tore it open and rolled it down over him, taking her time.

T-Rex growled and finished the job. Then he ran his hand over her buttocks and scooped her up by the backs of her thighs, wrapping her legs around his waist. Pressing her against the slick tiles of the shower wall, he kissed her hard, sliding his tongue into her mouth as his erection nudged her opening.

He lifted his head, dragging in a lungful of steadying air. "Tell me *no* now, if that's what you want."

"You're kidding, right?" Sierra shook her head and eased her body downward, taking him inside her. "I want you. Please, don't stop now."

Her channel welcomed him, wet, warm and tight around him.

He eased into her slowly, all the way, giving her

time to adjust to his girth. Once he was buried to the hilt, he asked, "Are you all right?"

"Oh, my," she said, her voice hitching. "More than all right. More, please."

He chuckled and pulled almost all the way out before reversing the direction.

"Harder," she whispered, wrapping her arms around his neck and tightening her legs around his waist. "Faster," she urged.

He thrust into her again and again, establishing a rhythm as ancient as time. But he held back, refusing to release. He wanted her with him when he did.

As the water grew colder, T-Rex steeled himself to withdraw and set Sierra on her feet.

"What? Why did you stop? I was almost there," she cried.

"I want you to enjoy this as much as I do," he said.

"I am," she said.

Still he rinsed them both, turned off the water and led her out of the tub onto the bath mat. With a warm, fluffy towel, he rubbed her skin dry.

Sierra returned the favor, lingering over his stiff erection. When she was done, she wrapped her towel around her body, while he wrapped his around his waist.

She took his hand and opened the door, poking her head out. "The coast is clear."

"My room or yours?" he asked.

"I don't care as long as we get there quickly." Tightening her hold on his fingers, she ran across the hall and pushed into her bedroom, dragging him in behind her.

T-Rex closed the door and twisted the lock. "Now I can show you how a lady should be made love to."

"I was counting on that," she said with a smile and let the towel around her drop to the floor.

SIERRA WATCHED AS T-Rex released his hold on his towel and the soft terry cloth fell, exposing the man's magnificent shaft, jutting out in front of him.

When he'd been inside her, she could barely breathe, he was so thick and…and…sweet love, he was so big. She couldn't wait to have him back inside her, filling that empty place she hadn't known ached for a man like him.

Taking his hand, she backed toward the bed. When the backs of her legs bumped into the mattress, she smiled. Oh, yes. This would be a night she'd remember for a very long time. She didn't want to waste a moment of it.

About to scoot her bottom up onto the bed, she was surprised when T-Rex swung her legs out from under her and laid her on the mattress.

She laughed. "I was getting there."

He stepped between her legs and leaned down

to capture her earlobe between his teeth. "I know. But you were taking too long. I have plans for you."

She widened her legs and leaned back on her elbows. "Plans? Sounds tempting." Sierra lowered her eyelids to half-mast, her heart pounding at the deep, sexy way he was talking. What could be more exciting than what he'd already done to her in the shower?

T-Rex dragged his lips across her chin to capture her mouth, sliding his tongue alongside hers in a slow, arousing caress. He didn't pause long, working his way down the column of her throat to the pulse beating wildly at the base of her neck.

She slid her hands over his impossibly broad shoulders, amazed at how hard the muscles were beneath his taut skin. Every move he made flexed them and made her want to touch his body all over.

T-Rex captured one of her breasts between his lips and rolled the tip until it hardened into a tight little bead. Then he moved to the other and lavished his attention on it.

Sierra arched off the bed, pressing her breast deeper into his mouth. He sucked hard on it and let go, trailing his mouth down her torso, alternately kissing, nipping and tonguing her skin as he moved lower. When he reached the tuft of hair over her sex, he paused to look up at her.

She felt as if she were perched on the edge of a precipice, waiting for him to draw her over.

He touched her entrance with the tip of his finger, sliding it into the warm, wet channel. Then he dragged it upward, parted her folds and slathered that little nubbin of flesh that held the key to her ultimate release. Swirling, stroking and flicking, he toyed with her until she was a writhing, moaning animal, twisting in the sheets.

If that wasn't enough to make her crazed with lust, he bent his head to her and flicked her with his tongue. There. In that very special place.

Sierra dug her heels into the mattress and came up off the bed, crying out, "Rex!"

He chuckled. "Like that?"

"Oh, my. Oh, my. Oh, my," she said, unable to form more coherent words when every nerve in her body was on fire with need. "Yes!"

Then he flicked her again and sucked her nubbin into his mouth, tonguing it over and over.

Sierra catapulted into the stratosphere, the tingling sensation graduating into lightning bolting through her from the molten core of her being to the very tips of her fingers.

As she rode the wave, she almost wanted to cry. This was right in so many ways. What T-Rex was doing to her was how it should always have been.

Before she came down from the incredibly beautiful high, she tugged on T-Rex's hair, urging him to come up her body and join her in the most intense pleasure she'd ever experienced.

He crawled up and settled between her legs. Then he kissed her and thrust deep inside her, filling her to full, prolonging her release to match his.

Again and again he thrust, until his body tensed, he thrust one last time and buried himself in her channel. His shaft throbbed inside her. He threw back his head and clenched his teeth so tightly his jaw twitched.

After a long, exquisite moment, Sierra floated back to earth.

T-Rex dropped down on top of her and rolled them both to their sides, his arms around her, pulling her close. He stroked her hair silently and held her until his breathing returned to normal.

Sierra burrowed into his muscular body and rested her hand on his chest. She'd promised not to expect commitment from him. But she couldn't imagine going through life without ever doing that again. The man could have ruined her for all others.

Chapter Twelve

T-Rex woke before sunrise, warm, content and naked. Lying in a strange room with Sierra's body snuggled up against his was just about as close to heaven as he could imagine.

He eased his arm out from under her and stared down at the woman lying in the bed beside him.

Her blond hair fanned out on the pillow, and her mouth turned up in a sexy smile as if she was dreaming about making love. To him.

He bent to gently brush a kiss across her forehead. He'd never made love to a woman with such intensity and desire. And she'd responded in kind, her cries as free and powerful as her release.

Her ex-husband had been a fool. This woman was kind, gentle and caring. But the passion hidden beneath her beautiful and soft exterior was everything a man could dream of. The man fortunate enough to capture her heart would be a lucky person indeed.

The urgent need to relieve himself reminded him

there was a world out there, and he'd be expected to join it soon. His only regret to the night before was that he'd have to get out of the bed and leave this woman for a day of hunting in the hills. He'd much prefer to remain in the warmth of her arms and make love to her all day long.

He slid from the bed, careful not to disturb her. Wrapping the towel around his waist, he left her room for his own, grabbed clothes and entered the bathroom. A quick, cold shower helped to reinforce his need to go to work, reducing his lusty thoughts enough he could think of the task ahead.

He would join the team in their search through the hills to find the cave with the cache of weapons. Unless the sheriff's department had captured them trying to leave the valley and relocate their store of rifles and whatever else they might have stashed away. He could always hope. Then he could stay where he was and spend the day in bed with Sierra.

But she had a job to do and a tour with the day care kids.

T-Rex sighed. Soon he was combed, dressed and ready to attack the day. When he pulled open the bathroom door, he almost ran into Sierra.

She stood in front of him, her hand raised to knock. Her beautiful long blond hair tumbled around her shoulders in wild abandon, but she had dressed in jeans and a long-sleeved blouse. Her cheeks turned a charming shade of pink, and she dipped her head. "Good morning."

T-Rex drew her into his arms and bent to nuzzle her ear. "Hey, beautiful."

"Ha. You're showered and shaved. I'm a mess."

"A gorgeous mess." He tipped her chin up and stared down into her eyes. "I wanted to stay in bed all day."

She sighed. "Me, too. But I promised Brenda I'd go with the moms and kids to the park at Yellowstone today."

"And you can't disappoint the kids." He bent to touch his lips to her forehead. "Need help scrubbing your back in the shower?" he whispered.

"Always." She cupped his face with her palm. "But you're all ready to go. I can manage on my own." She chewed on her bottom lip. "Will I see you at breakfast?"

He shook his head. "I have to meet the guys in ten minutes. That only gives me enough time to grab a cup of coffee." He frowned. "Are you sure you'll be all right at the park today?"

She nodded. "I'll be surrounded by the other ladies and the park rangers. Clay might be bold enough to attack me in front of a bunch of children who couldn't stop him. But surely he won't try anything in front of a bunch of adults."

"Yes, but he might try before you leave."

"I'll have Brenda pick me up in front of the bed-and-breakfast."

T-Rex nodded. "I'd like to be here to see you off." He glanced down at his watch. Eight minutes.

"Go." She touched his arm. "I'll be fine." Sierra grinned. "I'll carry the stun gun and a big rock, if it makes you feel any better."

He chuckled and pulled her into his arms, holding her tight. Then he claimed her lips in a kiss that felt like it could be their last.

Sierra wrapped her arms around his neck and returned the kiss, her breasts smashed against his chest, her belly pressing against his rising erection.

In need of air, he finally broke the kiss and rested his forehead against hers. "So much for cold showers."

She laughed, kissed him briefly and stepped out of his arms. "You have to go, and I need to get ready."

"Do you have my cell phone number?" he asked.

She shook her head.

"Give me your number." He pulled out his phone and entered her digits. Then he called it.

He could hear her phone ringing in her bedroom. "Now you'll have mine. Call me if you have any problems whatsoever."

"You'll be out in the hills and canyons. The call won't go through."

"I'll check my phone when I get back to town. I'll

also text the number for Hack. He's always in the office. He can relay messages to me in the field. We'll carry radios to communicate."

She rested a hand on his chest. "Be careful out there."

He captured her hand in his, raised it to his lips and pressed a kiss into her palm. "You be careful at Yellowstone. I hear the buffalo can be aggressive."

Sierra snorted. "They are the least of my worries. I'll have half a dozen children around my feet wanting to pet them."

"You'll do great. Those kids love you."

She smiled. "I love them, too. Now, go, or we'll be here all day."

He turned and descended the stairs to the first floor.

Mrs. McCall held up a pot of coffee in the dining room. "Need one to go?"

"I'd love one," he answered.

"Everything all right?" Mrs. McCall asked as she handed him an insulated disposable cup filled with steaming black coffee.

"Couldn't be better." He took the cup and pressed a lid onto it. "Why do you ask?"

"I just wondered if you were tired this morning. What with all the racket last night." She didn't meet his gaze, but her lips curled upward in a smile. "That Sierra Daniels is a sweetheart. Always good to everyone. She certainly didn't deserve to be treated the way her ex-husband treated her."

"No, she didn't. And yes, she is a sweet lady."

Mrs. McCall met his gaze, her smile gone. "Sure would hate to see her hurt again."

T-Rex swallowed the piping-hot coffee he'd just sipped and nearly gagged on the heat burning its way down his throat. He sputtered and blew out a stream of hot air before responding to the older woman. "I'd hate to see her hurt, as well." Then, quickly, before the woman could give him more advice about Sierra, he left the dining room and hurried out the door to his truck.

Although he'd left the bed-and-breakfast, he couldn't seem to leave Mrs. McCall's words behind.

Sierra Daniels deserved to be happy. Though their lovemaking had been the result of mutual consent, T-Rex suspected it would leave her hurt in the long run. He'd leave, she'd be alone and her ex-husband would still be around to harass her.

A few days ago, all T-Rex could think about was leaving Grizzly Pass. Now all he could think about was what he'd be leaving behind. He no longer had the burning desire to return to his unit and seek revenge on the faceless enemy who'd crippled Gunny and killed other members of his team.

There were people right there in the United States

who needed help. Innocents like Sierra and the children she was responsible for.

T-Rex had a lot to think about while he searched the hills for the homegrown terrorists.

SIERRA SHOWERED, DRESSED in a crisp, clean pair of jeans, a long-sleeved blouse and a sweater. After being so very cold the day before, she grabbed a jacket to take along, in case the temperature dropped or they were unexpectedly delayed in their return to Grizzly Pass.

She called Brenda, who agreed to swing by and collect her before meeting the other moms who would caravan out to the Old Faithful Visitor Education Center at Yellowstone. They had arranged for a park ranger to give the children a guided tour, explaining the ecosystem and the most interesting facts about the ancient volcano simmering beneath the surface. It would be a fun, educational trip for the children, one they'd looked forward to for over a month.

Too bad Sierra didn't feel much like going. She'd rather be out in the hills with the Safe Haven team searching for the men who'd shot down their helicopter yesterday. That wasn't exactly the truth. She wanted to be with T-Rex, whatever he was doing in the hills.

She eventually descended the staircase and joined

Mrs. McCall in the dining room. They were the only two people at the table.

"Were there no other guests in the bed-and-breakfast last night?" Sierra asked.

The older woman shook her head. "No. Just you and Mr. Trainor. I expect a couple to show up some time this afternoon. But they're only staying the night before moving on."

Heat rose in Sierra's cheeks. If there were no other guests, had the establishment's owner heard the noises coming from her room last night?

Mrs. McCall reached across the table and patted her hand. "Sierra, sweetie, I've known you a long time. Your foster mother and I used to be in the same quilting club. I've watched you grow from a little girl with pigtails into the beautiful young woman you are now."

Sierra choked on the tea she'd been sipping and set the cup on the table. "Thank you, Mrs. McCall." She wondered where the woman would go with the conversation.

"I can see you are falling in love with Mr. Trainor."

Sierra gasped and shook her head. "No, Mrs. McCall. We've only known each other a couple of days. It would be impossible to fall in love that quickly."

Mrs. McCall gave her a knowing smile. "Sweetie,

I knew I loved my Henry the moment we met. It just took him a little longer to realize he loved me, too."

Sierra's eyes stung. She blinked and looked down at her hand holding the teacup. "Really, I'm not in love. Mr. Trainor isn't going to be in Grizzly Pass for long. When his mission is complete, he'll be on his way back to his unit."

"Sierra, it's not too late. You still have time to show him that he is capable of love. He doesn't know it, but he's halfway there now."

Sierra raised her glance to the bed-and-breakfast owner. "It's impossible. He's career military. He's leaving."

"So?" Mrs. McCall rose from her chair and collected the empty plates. "You have nothing holding you back. I'm sure your foster parents would have wanted you to get out of this little town, spread your wings and experience more of the world."

"If I wanted to, I could do it on my own." Sierra stood and helped clear the table, walking into the kitchen behind the older woman. "I don't need a man with me in order to experience the world."

Mrs. McCall nodded. "True. But if there's a special man, one who understands you, treats you right and loves you, isn't the experience richer?" She set the plates in the sink and turned to take the biscuit basket from Sierra's hand. "Think about it, will you?"

Sierra wanted to tell her she'd thought about all

of those things and come back to the promise she'd made T-Rex. She wouldn't look for commitment. What they'd done last night was supposed to be a one-night stand. *The end*.

But she couldn't quite tack those two words onto what she was feeling. She couldn't believe last night was the end. Mrs. McCall was right about one thing. She still had time. Time to be with T-Rex until he left. If he left without looking back, then she would add the two words to what they'd had and move on.

She might even decide to leave Grizzly Pass and see the world. Maybe there was a rich family looking for a nanny to travel with them. Or she could go back to school, finish her degree and find a job in another state as a teacher. The sky was the limit.

Sierra checked the clock. Brenda would be there in a few minutes, and she was still mooning over a man who'd made it clear he wasn't sticking around, nor was he the kind of man who needed or wanted a woman to follow him from post to post.

Straightening her shoulders, Sierra decided she'd take every minute she had with him and ask no more. In the meantime, she had a field trip to go on and she wasn't ready. She ran up the stairs to the bathroom, brushed her teeth and grabbed her jacket and purse. When she came back down, Brenda was pulling up in front of the bed-and-breakfast.

Before Sierra stepped out of the building, she

checked for any sign of Clay. His truck wasn't anywhere in sight. Breathing a sigh of relief, she left the building and climbed into Brenda's SUV.

"Well, look at you all chipper this morning." Brenda shifted into gear and drove toward the community center. "How was your date with the marine yesterday?"

Sierra's cheeks burned, and she couldn't meet her friend's gaze.

"Oh, my God. You hooked up with him!" Brenda squealed in delight.

"What?" Sierra shot a glance her way. "I did not—"

"Oh, baby, don't even bother to deny it. Your lips are puffy, and you have a little beard burn on your cheek. At the very least you were thoroughly kissed. But the way you're blushing, it was a lot more than that."

Sierra gave up and sagged against the seat, a smile pulling her lips upward. "Yesterday was the best day of my life."

"Tell me all," Brenda insisted, her face animated. "Hurry, before we load up with kids. I want all of the lovely details."

"Well, other than the helicopter crash and being shot at, I'd say it went pretty well."

Brenda slammed her foot onto the brake pedal. "What?"

Sierra caught herself before hitting the dash.

"You didn't hear? I would have thought the grape-vine would have had it all over the county by now."

"You forget, I live alone."

"That never stopped anyone from spreading the most interesting gossip far and wide among the Beartooth Mountains." Sierra laughed and started from the beginning, giving a brief summation of what had happened up to the moment she and T-Rex arrived back at the bed-and-breakfast. "And that's what you missed."

"Oh, darlin', you're not stopping there." Brenda pulled up to the community center. "I want the rest. Give it to me. Quickly, because we're here and the kiddos are waiting."

"Sorry. We're being waved over." Sierra grinned and climbed out of the vehicle.

"Oh, that is so not fair." Brenda shook her head. "He must have been spectacular."

"Beyond," Sierra said, letting her smile broaden as she approached the mothers and small children who would be coming along for the field trip.

Sierra and Brenda would take three kids and two mothers in Brenda's SUV with seating for seven. Two other mothers would follow in a Suburban with another five children whose ages ranged from four to six.

The trip took only an hour and fifteen minutes when one drove the speed limit. But the roads were curvy. To avoid the usual carsickness, they took the curves very slowly and entertained the children with songs and games to keep them occupied.

When they rolled into the parking lot of the Old Faithful Visitor Education Center, the children were ready to get out and stretch their little legs.

"Why is the parking lot so full?" Brenda shifted into Park and got out. "I mean it's not even time for Old Faithful to blow."

Sierra climbed out of the vehicle and glanced around at the vehicles crammed into the lot and the vans with satellite antennas and the lettering of local television stations written on the sides. Then it came to her. "I forgot. Grady Morris is supposed to be here today for a campaign speech."

"Oh, yeah. Last night on the news, they said he'd have a special guest with him." Brenda tilted her head. "I wonder who it is."

"Based on the number of black SUVs and men in black suits, it has to be a very important person," Sierra said.

The other two mothers and their children joined them. "Should we call off this excursion?" one of them said.

"It's awfully crowded," noted another.

"We're here," Sierra said. "We might as well check it out. Maybe our tour guide will get us out on the trails before this shindig kicks off."

The women herded the children through the

parked cars, past several men in black clothing and black sunglasses, their jackets bulging. Probably with a weapon or two each.

The lobby was full of people, jostling each other. More men in suits and reporters with cameras and microphones.

"I've been here on a number of occasions when this place was teeming with tourists, but this is crazy," Brenda said.

Sierra nodded. "Let's just hope it's not as packed inside as it is out front."

They were disappointed to learn it was even more crowded in the center.

"Stay here," Sierra said. "I'll make my way to the desk and see if I can find our park ranger tour guide."

Brenda and the mothers backed the children into an empty corner and waited.

Sierra waded through the crowd to the desk and stood in a line seven people deep. By the time she reached the desk, she was ready to call the whole event off. The noise level had grown into a dull roar inside the building. It was giving her a headache and touch of agoraphobia. She didn't much care for large crowds.

"How may I help you?" The perky young woman behind the counter pushed a strand of hair back behind her ear.

"We made prior arrangements for the ranger-led activities."

The woman keyed into the computer. "Group name?"

"Grizzly Pass Mother's Day Out."

The noise in the room increased to a fevered pitch, and one of the counter clerks pointed. "There he is. The vice president of the United States."

Sierra spun in time to catch a glimpse of the vice president, flanked by Secret Service men, being hustled through the crowd from a back room and out the door of the building, leading to the geyser viewing area. The crowd outside cheered. Through the glass doors, Sierra could see Grady Morris standing on a raised stage, shaking hands with the vice president.

"You'll have Ranger Jared today," the clerk said, drawing Sierra's attention back to the counter.

"Is that really the vice president of the United States?" Sierra asked.

The young lady puffed out her chest, her eyes bright with excitement. "Yes, ma'am."

"Did you know he'd be here?" Sierra asked.

She beamed. "We didn't know until right before we left work last night. We all had to come in early and clean like crazy to be ready for him this morning. And they built the stage out by Old Faithful in less than two hours. It was amazing." The woman looked behind her. "Oh, here's Ranger Jared. He'll take you to the exhibits room, unless you want to stand outside and watch the show first."

"No. The children are much too young to understand a campaign speech."

Ranger Jared glanced over the heads of the crowd. "I've never seen it like this. It's insane."

"You're telling me. Should we postpone and come back when it's not this crowded?" Sierra asked.

"No. No. This crowd won't be interested in the discovery room. We'll probably have it all to ourselves with everyone else outside. Come on back."

Sierra gathered the women and children and led them through the door where Ranger Jared stood.

He was right. The crowd had moved out to the geyser viewing area where the stage had been erected. Soon he had the kids engaged in learning about geysers, hot springs and more.

The children were happy to touch and explore the indoor exhibits and momentarily would be led outdoors to see some of the real deals on the trails.

Ranger Jared clapped his hands to get their attention. "If you will all step across the lobby into the theater, we have a little show we'd like you to see before we go outside. Follow me." He led the way back through the lobby and into the theater.

Sierra helped guide the small children into seats near the front of the room. Once they were all in place, she stood to the side, leaning against the wall.

The lights dimmed and the film began. It was all about the ecosystem of the park and how the volcano had come to be, how it had erupted and created a warm place for the animals to gather around during the cold months of the year. The narrator talked of the different species of animals that roamed the park, including bison, deer, elk, black bears, grizzly bears and the wolves that had been reintroduced.

Even Sierra was caught up in the video. The theater walls were soundproofed. The people outside the theater couldn't hear what was going on inside and vice versa. So she was surprised when someone burst through the door and yelled, "Get down on the floor and don't move or we'll shoot!"

With the doors open, she could hear the sounds of screaming and shouting and the crack of gunfire.

Sierra, her heart pounding, ran toward the children. "Get on the floor," she yelled. "Get down!"

Gunfire ripped through the theater.

"I said get down!" A man in a ski mask brandished a military-grade rifle in the air. "That means you, Blondie!"

The children screamed and cried. Most of them slid out of their seats and lay on the floor. One little boy sat petrified in his theater seat, too young to understand what was going on and too frightened to move.

Sierra dropped to her hands and knees and

crawled to the boy, scooped him out of his seat and onto the ground, hunkering over him to block any bullets that might be fired in their direction.

"In here!" the gunman shouted. "Bring them in here!"

Sierra lifted her head high enough to peer over the seats at the upper end of the theater. Two men in business suits were shoved through the door by a group of men dressed in camouflage and ski masks.

"Down in front." One of the men waved his rifle at the others. "Take them down in front where we can see them. And turn on the lights. It's too dark in here."

A man in a ski mask kicked Ranger Jared in the side. "You. Get the lights on. Now!"

Jared staggered to his feet and hurried to the controls on the wall. He flipped several switches, and the lights grew brighter. As soon as he was done, he was shoved back down the aisle to where Sierra and the other women were hovering over the children.

The little ones sobbed, their cries getting louder with all of the shouting. It didn't help that one of the mothers was losing it in front of the kids.

"We're going to die. We're going to die," she kept saying.

"Lady, shut up, or you will," a man carrying a rifle said.

"Shh, Laura. We're going to be fine. Just keep your cool for the children," Sierra said.

Beside her Brenda shook, her teeth chattering. Not a week earlier, the woman had been in a bus hijacking. If anyone had a right to lose it, it was Brenda.

But Sierra couldn't, not when the children depended on her to see them safely home.

Chapter Thirteen

T-Rex met up with Ghost and Caveman in front of the Blue Moose Tavern. Garner hurried down the stairs, carrying what appeared to be two duffel bags.

"We're meeting Hawkeye at the Stone Oak Ranch and taking the four-wheelers from there."

"Whatcha got?" T-Rex asked.

"The armory." Garner laid the heavy bags in the back of his SUV. "M4A1 rifles, radio headsets and Kevlar vests. We're not going unarmed or un-prepared."

T-Rex snorted. "Glad to hear it. I felt at a distinct disadvantage yesterday in the hills."

Garner's lips thinned. "We didn't plan on having a helicopter shot down."

"No, we didn't," T-Rex agreed and closed the hatch.

"How soon will the FAA be out to investigate the crash site?" Ghost asked.

"They're on their way now." Garner climbed into

the driver's seat and twisted the key in the ignition. "Should be here before noon. All the more reason to find that cave and neutralize any bad guys before they stir up any more trouble." He glanced at the rest of them. "Are you coming, or not?"

The three men jumped into the SUV and held on while Garner sped out of town.

"What about the sheriff?" T-Rex glanced up at the hills. They appeared so serene, as though they couldn't possibly harbor a bunch of terrorists. "Any activity on the roads last night?"

"His men didn't see anything moving," Garner answered. "The one truck he stopped was a man on his way to the airport in Bozeman. No weapons stashed in his backseat or truck bed."

"I can't imagine them leaving their weapons cache in the cave." T-Rex shook his head. "Not after shooting down a military helicopter."

"The Army National Guard sent another Black Hawk. The pilot and copilot are waiting at the fairgrounds. The ship is armed to the teeth. The guard is angry about losing one of their birds. I barely got them to wait. I don't want to start an all-out war and get people killed who actually belong on the neighboring ranches. I told them to give us the morning to find the cave and attack it from the ground."

"I'm surprised they agreed," Ghost said.

Garner shrugged. "I had help from their higher headquarters."

"Will the sheriff's department be with us on this venture?" Caveman asked.

"They will. The sheriff, along with seven of his finest deputies and members of the Wyoming State Police, will be combing the hills alongside us."

T-Rex shook his head. "Sounds like this could turn out to be a goat rope."

"Can't be helped." Garner's hands tightened on the steering wheel. "We need the manpower to search the caves. If there are more than thirty AR-15s up there, it stands to reason there could be thirty men using them." Garner shot a glance at T-Rex in the front seat. "I'll take all the help we can get."

Caveman leaned over the back of Garner's seat. "How is everyone getting up into the hills?"

"We're taking the four-wheelers we left at the Stone Oak Ranch." Garner left Grizzly Pass and headed south. "The sheriff department has their own fleet of four-wheelers, and I have no idea what the state police will bring. All I know is we need to find these bastards and take them down before they hurt anyone else. Oh, and several of the folks we had on our list of possible members of Free America called in sick or didn't show up to work today."

"How'd you find out?"

"I had feelers out to their employers. They notified me as soon as the calls came in or the men didn't arrive on time."

T-Rex's hands balled into fists. Things could get real ugly real fast. "How many?"

"Nine that we know about, so far," Garner said.

"Sounds like they might be mobilizing," Caveman cursed. "Why couldn't we bring any of them in earlier?"

"We didn't have any evidence." Garner glanced in his rearview mirror at the men in the seat behind him. "Ghost, you and Caveman followed some of them, and they didn't lead you anywhere but to their homes."

"Damned waste of time," Ghost grumbled. "If we could have interrogated them, we'd have had more to go on."

"What about Rausch? Has he talked?" T-Rex asked.

"The sheriff is meeting us at the ranch," Garner said. "Hopefully, he has news on that front." He glanced in his rearview mirror again. "If I'm not mistaken, that's him behind us now."

They arrived at Stone Oak Ranch and met Olivia at the house.

Several vehicles pulled into the driveway behind them, including four from the sheriff's department and three from the state police. They had trailers attached filled with four-wheelers.

Olivia and Hawkeye met them with contour maps of the area. They spread them over the hood of Garner's vehicle, and the team gathered around along with the law enforcement personnel. They determined the approximate location of the cave from which the rocket had been shot, assigned areas to each team and took off.

Because the Safe Haven team had been the most recent to visit the area, they led the pack.

T-Rex insisted on taking point. As he drove the roads to the narrowing trails up into the hills, he couldn't help thinking about Sierra. Was she all right? Had Ellis shown up that morning to cause problems? Or was her ex-husband with the Free America group, preparing to take over the world?

He wished he could be in two places at once. Alas, he couldn't and his job was exactly where he was.

As they neared the valley lined with caves, he slowed his ATV and pulled out a pair of binoculars. His team stopped even with him and did the same.

"Is that metal?" Hawkeye asked, pointing to one of the caves. "There. The third cave from the end. The one with the tire tracks leading up to it. Is that a metal ammo box on the edge of the entrance?"

T-Rex trained his binoculars at the third cave from the end of the valley. Just as Hawkeye had said, there was a metal ammo box lying on its side near the mouth of the cave. T-Rex dismounted, pulled the M4 rifle from the scabbard and waited for the others to catch up.

Garner organized the sheriff's deputies and state police into an assault team to follow the Safe Haven men into battle.

T-Rex led the charge, hugging the shadows of the trees, moving closer a little at a time. Soon he was standing below the cave in the shade of a lodgepole pine, staring up at an empty ammo can. Nothing moved on the trail or in the dimness of the cave. Nothing that he could see.

Ghost came up to stand beside him. "Anything?"

"I'd bet this was the cave. I'd also bet it's empty of the people who were there yesterday."

"Let's find out. Cover me." Ghost passed T-Rex and started up the hill.

T-Rex followed.

At the entrance to the cave, they paused, inching up from the side, out of sight and range of anyone aiming a rifle their direction.

T-Rex poked his head around the side of the rock wall and peered into the darkness. Nothing moved. "Ready?" he said. "Cover me."

He took three steps into the darkness and felt something across his ankle. T-Rex froze and yelled, "Get back! This place is rigged!"

Since he hadn't triggered the detonator, he knew that if he moved his ankle now, he'd set off the explosion. He waited for Ghost to get back behind the safety of the rock wall. Then, taking a deep breath, T-Rex threw himself in that direction, somersaulted and rolled to his feet.

An explosion knocked him over and sent him tumbling down the hillside to the valley floor. He lay for a long time, his ears ringing, unable to take a breath. Dust flew all around him, dimming the light from the sun above.

Caveman appeared over him. "T-Rex!" He seemed to be shouting, but the sound barely made it to him. "T-Rex, breathe!" He pushed on his chest and forced air out.

T-Rex gasped and sucked in a lungful of dusty air. He sat up coughing, breathing as deeply as he could to fill his empty lungs. After popping his ears several times, he could hear better, but the ringing continued.

"They rigged it. They had a trip wire just inside the cave where you couldn't see it." T-Rex held up his hand. "Help me up."

Caveman grabbed his hand and pulled him to his feet. "Are you all right?"

"I have to be. If they aren't here, they have to be somewhere else. From what I could see before I set off the explosion, there were empty ammo cases, tables and chairs and maps on the walls."

"Could you tell what the maps were of?" Garner asked.

"No. I couldn't see that much. My eyes hadn't adjusted completely to the dark interior before the explosion." T-Rex covered his ears and pressed hard, hoping to readjust his eardrums. It helped, but he still heard sounds as if they were coming from the end of a long tunnel. And that damned ringing wouldn't stop.

Caveman and Ghost climbed the hill to the cave and pulled at a few rocks before shaking their heads and coming back down.

Sheriff Scott had joined them. "I'll see what I can do to get a crew out here to dig that cave out. There has to be something in there they're trying to hide. We might be able to pull fingerprints from whatever is left of the cases and ammo boxes."

Ghost pointed to the ammo box they'd passed on their way up before the explosion. "You might get something from that one. And you won't have to dig to do it."

The sheriff nodded. "I sent my men and the state police north following the trail to see if they find where they moved the goods. If you're up to it, you might want to follow. There are a lot of trails and roads leading into and out of these hills. Just because my men didn't see anyone on the roads last night, doesn't mean they didn't leave. But then again, they might still be holed up in an alternate location."

"We'll follow," T-Rex said. To him, his voice

sounded as if he was speaking from a long way away. He started toward his four-wheeler.

Garner caught his arm and pulled him to a halt. "I think you should go back to the ranch house. You took quite a tumble, and that explosion probably didn't do your eardrums or anything else any good."

"I'm fine."

Garner held up two fingers. "How many fingers am I holding up?"

"Two." He frowned at his temporary boss. "Can we go now?"

Garner nodded. "Yes. But for the record, I don't like it. I think you should see a doctor."

"Later. We have a small army to stop."

They followed the others along the trail. Soon, T-Rex's head cleared enough to realize they were nearing the valley where the pipeline inspector had been killed.

As he rolled over the top of the ridge and came to a halt, he looked down at the trail leading to the bottom. The law enforcement officers were almost to the bottom. When they left the trail and drove across the valley floor, another explosion rocked the ground. Rocks and dust blasted into the air from the area around the pipeline.

The deputy in front of the pack flipped over the handlebars of his four-wheeler and landed a couple of yards away. The two ATV riders behind him swerved and flipped their four-wheelers. Those behind them stopped suddenly, leaped from their vehicles and ran toward the downed men.

From his perch high above, T-Rex stared down at the chaos and commotion. He glanced all around, from the top of the other ridge down the sides of the hills to the bottom. Nothing else moved. Not a single member of the Free America group stood around to watch the explosion here or at the cave. It was almost as if they'd known someone would come that way looking for them and they set up a smoke screen to hide what they were really up to.

Garner pulled his ATV up beside T-Rex and jerked the radio from the pocket of his jacket. "Garner here."

"It's me, Hack," the computer guy's voice crackled over the radio.

"Yeah, what's wrong?" Garner asked.

"Got trouble up north. You're wasting your time looking for your Free America group in the hills. They've staged their takeover."

T-Rex left his vehicle and crossed to where Garner stood.

"Where?" Garner demanded.

"At Old Faithful. They're at the visitors center. There was a campaign rally there today with Grady Morris. He had a surprise visitor with him."

"Who?" Garner asked.

"The vice president of the United States."

A lead weight settled low in T-Rex's belly. *Holy hell.* And then his gut twisted into a tight knot. "Sierra Daniels was going to Yellowstone today. They were supposed to be at Old Faithful today."

"Anyone else caught in the takeover?" Garner asked into the radio.

Hack replied, "Some women and little kids who were in the theater where they took the vice president. They think half a dozen women and half a dozen children were in there. Something like seventeen people are being held hostage."

"What's going on?" Ghost stepped up beside T-Rex.

T-Rex clenched his fists. "This whole effort today was a waste of time, a smoke screen for what they were planning."

"And what was that?" Ghost asked.

"They've taken hostages at the Old Faithful visitors center. The vice president is one of them."

Caveman joined them. "Vice president of what?"

T-Rex turned to his teammates. "Of the United States of America." He hurried toward his ATV.

"Where are you going?" Garner asked.

"Sierra Daniels was there." He threw his leg over the seat and started the engine. "I have a sinking feeling she's among the hostages, along with the children in her care. I'm going to rescue her."

SIERRA HUDDLED ON the floor with the other women, holding the little ones in her arms, trying to comfort them and keep them quiet. The armed men who'd taken them and the vice president of the United States hostage didn't look like they'd put up with much. Crying children would only make them angry and impatient.

They'd been held in the theater for over an hour without any idea of what the group was demanding. Some of the children had cried themselves to sleep. Others clung to the adults, hiding their faces from the bad guys. It wouldn't be long before they got hungry or had to use the bathroom. The crying would start all over again.

Sierra handed Brenda the little boy she'd been holding and stood.

"Where are you going?" Brenda asked, her brows furrowed, the strain of the takeover showing in the lines around her mouth.

"To find out what's going on and try to negotiate the children's release."

"You can't." Brenda grabbed her hand. "You heard them. They'll shoot anyone standing."

"You two, shut up and sit down," a voice said.

Another masked man entered the room behind the bossy one. "I'm taking over here," he said. "You can join the others outside in the lobby."

"I was told not to leave them," Bossy Man argued.

The man grabbed Bossy Man by the collar and shoved him toward the door. "Get the hell out! Now!"

Sierra recognized the voice and fought the sinking feeling in her belly. She'd heard that same tone too often over the past eight years. The man staring through the slits in a ski mask was her ex-husband, Clay Ellis.

Once the other man was gone, Clay started toward her. The other guard standing watch over the vice president and Grady Morris called out, "What are you doing?"

"Our leader wanted names of the hostages."

The man snorted. "He has the most important one. No one tops the vice president except the president himself."

"Look here, young man." The vice president rose from the theater seat and took a step toward his captor. "Release us at once before this goes too far."

The man turned his weapon on the vice president and said in a cold, deadly tone, "Move one more step and I'll blow a hole right through you."

"You don't want to do that. Murder carries a lot longer sentence than kidnapping. In some states a murderer can get the death penalty. Don't go there, son."

"I'm not your son," the man spit at the country's second in command. "Don't tell me where to go or what to do. I know my chances of getting out of this alive are nil. Why should I care if I take a few people out with me?"

"Please, Mr. Vice President. Sit down," Sierra said. The last thing she wanted to see or have the children witness was the murder of the vice president or anyone else, for that matter.

The vice president backed up and took his seat.

Clay's counterpart aimed his rifle at Sierra. "Now, you sit down and shut up."

"Back off. I've got this one," Clay said. He walked all of the way down to where Sierra stood, grabbed her arm and dragged her away from the others. "Play your cards right and I'll get you out of here."

"I know it's you, Clay. That mask hides nothing from me," Sierra said, her tone low. "You can't let them do this."

"It's too late. We're in this now, and we're not going home."

"What does that mean?"

"Just what I said. We won't be going home from here. Once those in charge have their say in front of a billion Americans, we're going to scatter to the winds. I won't be going back to Grizzly Pass. And you're coming with me."

"Okay."

He squeezed her arm tighter. "Okay? Why the big turnaround now? Have a change of heart? Afraid of me at last?"

"I'll go with you. But I have one condition," Sierra said. This might be her only angle to get the terrorists to release the children. She had to play the card she'd been dealt.

"You're not in a position to demand conditions," he said.

"If you don't grant my condition, I won't go with you willingly. If you grant it, I will go with you and cause you no trouble."

His eyes narrowed in the slits of the mask. "What condition?"

"Release the children."

"No way. They're a bargaining chip."

"You have the biggest bargaining chip with the vice president of the United States. What more do you need? He draws more attention to the media than a handful of kids who will be screaming again as soon as they get hungry or have to go to the bathroom."

"Why should I trust you?" he said. "How do I know you won't go back on your word?"

"I'm not the one who lied and cheated in our relationship."

"You lied when you said until death do us part."

"I didn't lie. I was no longer married to the same man. He died somewhere in the past eight years. Whereas you lied when you said you'd love, honor and cherish me. What part of beating your wife is cherishing?"

His lips pulled back in a snarl. "If you weren't so damned mouthy…"

"It didn't matter if I talked or was mute. You hit me. And if I go with you again, you'll hit me again."

His eyes narrowed again. "So why would you promise to go with me, then?"

Sierra pushed back her shoulders and lifted her chin. "Because I care more for those children than I do for myself. They're just starting their lives. They deserve a chance to live them."

"I'm not in charge. I can't promise anything. But if it means you'll come with me without an argument, it might just be worth it." He shoved her back toward the women and children. "For now, sit down and shut up."

Sierra did as she was told, sinking onto the floor beside Brenda.

Clay walked back up to the exit. "I'll be right back."

"Yeah. That's right. Leave me with all of these hostages. At least give me enough bullets to take care of all of them."

Clay pulled a thirty-round curved magazine from a strap on his vest and tossed it to the man standing guard over the vice president. "Shoot them if they give you any trouble."

The man sneered. "Even your wife?"

Clay shot a killer glance at Sierra. "Especially my wife." Then he left the room, closing the door behind him.

If Sierra hoped to get out of the situation, she had to come up with a plan. She had no intention of going with Clay Ellis anywhere. The man was on a one-way path to hell, and he could damn well get there by himself. But she had the children to think of. If she could negotiate their release, she'd tell the devil anything he wanted to hear.

Chapter Fourteen

Thankfully, the Black Hawk waiting at the fairgrounds was large enough to carry the entire Safe
Haven team and their weapons to Yellowstone National Park. The state police, county sheriff's department and the National Guard had been alerted and
were on their way. Some of the county sheriff's deputies were there, herding tourists out of harm's way.

Garner was on the radio with Hack and the county
sheriff the entire way there, keeping apprised of the
situation. As they approached a field close to the Old
Faithful Visitor Education Center, Garner turned to
the others.

"There are approximately twenty heavily armed
Free America members at the visitors center. Ten inside and ten outside." Garner stared at the four men.
"Since they don't have a SWAT team available or
on-site, I've asked if they would like for our highly
trained combat team to be the ones to go in and neu-

tralize the situation. Right now, they have a hostage negotiator working with the FA people."

"What do they want?"

"They want to make a big splash in the news. They've asked for news teams from the big networks. When they're done making their speech, they want helicopters to take them to the border of US and Canada. Only then will they release the hostages."

"Seventeen unarmed hostages and twenty bad guys armed to the teeth?" T-Rex shook his head. "Even they can't be serious. That's a transportation nightmare. And Canada will refuse to allow them in. They have to know they are on a suicide mission."

Garner's lips pressed into a thin line. "My bet is they'll wait until the news teams are in place and then they'll make their big announcement and martyr themselves and their captives."

"Should we wait and see if they can negotiate the release of the hostages?" Caveman asked. "We're not in the Middle East. If we go storming in, there could be civilian casualties."

Garner nodded. "If we go in, we have to go in stealth mode. We can't go in shooting from the hip and raising hell." He touched his headset. "Hold on. Hack's talking."

He bent his head and cupped his hand over his

headset, nodding as he listened. When he glanced up, he smiled. "They've released eight children."

"Was that all of the kids?"

"The park rangers seem to think they were all part of a ranger-led group. There were eight children, six women and a ranger in the group."

T-Rex leaned forward. "Did they release any of the women?"

Garner nodded again. "Two women, identified as mothers, were released with the children. They kept four of the women, the ranger, vice president and Grady Morris." His gaze captured T-Rex's. "They said they'd start shooting captives if they don't get those news crews in the next fifteen minutes. They'll start with the women."

T-Rex cursed and willed the helicopter to land faster. He understood the need to touch down out of range of the terrorists and potential rocket-propelled grenades. The Wyoming National Guard wouldn't want to risk losing another expensive helicopter through careless mistakes. But damn. Could they put the craft on the ground already?

His hand on the release clips of his harness, T-Rex counted the seconds until the helicopter skids kissed the dirt. He unclipped his harness, shucked his headset and jumped to the ground.

"T-Rex." Garner was right behind him with a hand

on his arm. "You can't go charging in without assessing the situation and coming up with a plan."

"We can't wait until they start shooting the hostages."

"We have at least ten minutes before that happens. Ten minutes to get in and rescue them." Garner's hand tightened on T-Rex's arm. "We don't want to make them nervous and start shooting hostages sooner."

T-Rex drew in a deep breath and let it out slowly. Garner was right. "I won't let them kill Sierra."

"Or the vice president," Ghost added. "We don't want any of those people shot. We need to study the situation and come up with a plan."

His teeth grinding together, his jaw tight, T-Rex nodded. His teammates were right. "Time's running out. Let's get somewhere we can see what's going on."

The team grabbed the rifles Garner had packed into the duffel bag, checked the full magazines and slipped into the protective vests Garner had included. The rifles were equipped with silencers, which would come in handy if they wanted to take out certain bad guys and not alert the others. They were also given radio headsets for communication among the team members.

Meanwhile, Garner coordinated with the law enforcement team currently positioned in the parking lot. He informed them they would be swinging around from the side and to hold their fire.

"I'm having the law enforcement crew clear the parking lot. The helicopter pilot will move closer, providing a distraction while we move in from behind."

The team moved through the trees surrounding the visitors center on two sides. When they were close enough, T-Rex took the lead and crossed to one of the outer buildings separate from the larger main building.

"There's a man in the prone position on each corner of this end of the building."

"Can you sneak up on them?"

T-Rex studied all angles. He'd have to cross an area that would leave him exposed and alert the guards. He wouldn't make it without being seen. "I don't think so. If I step out now, they'll see me and open fire."

"That will alert the rest of them, and they might start shooting prisoners," Ghost said.

At that moment, three bison wandered past close to his position, heading toward the main building.

"Wait," T-Rex said. "I have an idea." He slipped the sling of his weapon over his shoulder and waited until the second bison was within five feet of him. Then he ran to get on the opposite side of the animal, hunkered low and walked with the big beast to the edge of the building, past the enemy guard on the corner. Once past the man, he left the bison and ran for the side of the building, hugging the shadows.

"Be ready," he whispered into his mic. He slipped his knife from the scabbard on his belt and crept up behind the man on the corner. He was almost on him when another bison loped out in front of the guard, capturing the man's attention.

T-Rex grabbed the guard by his boots, yanked him backward, out of sight of his counterpart, and slammed his head into the side of the building. The man fell limp to the ground.

T-Rex removed the bolt from his weapon and tied the guard's wrists with his own belt. Then he shoved the man's ski mask into his mouth. He didn't have much time.

A door on the side of the building gave him hope, until he tried it. It was locked. He shoved his knife between the door and the frame and jiggled it. He'd never unlocked a door like this before, but now would be the time to figure it out, since he was fresh out of hairpins or nail files.

He held his breath and jiggled the knife again. The lock sprang free, and the door swung open into a storage area stacked with boxes. Based on what Garner had briefed, the theater was on the end of the building he had entered. If he could get past the men on the inside, he might be able to sneak the prisoners out through one of the side doors. "I'm inside."

"The helicopter is on its way over. Ghost is making his move on the other guard."

"I can't wait. He can come through the door I left open. I'm going to check out the inside situation."

"Don't do anything rash until we're all inside," warned Garner.

T-Rex ignored Garner. He'd do what he had to in order to save Sierra. Glancing at his watch, he'd used five of the ten minutes he was working with. He inched his way through the storeroom to the door he presumed would lead into the bookstore or a hallway. He turned the knob and eased the door open toward him.

A man stood on the other side with his back to T-Rex.

T-Rex could see the lobby to the right. In his narrow view through the door, he counted four men armed with AR-15s standing to the sides out of range of potential snipers, all staring out toward the parking lot. The thumping of rotors could be heard as the helicopter hovered in the parking lot, making a slow landing to buy the team more distraction time.

T-Rex couldn't see anything to the left. He'd have to take a chance there weren't any other men close to the guy in front of him.

"I'm right behind you," Ghost whispered into his headset. "Invite the man in."

T-Rex reached out, slid his knife through the man's jugular, wrapped his arm around him and yanked him into the storeroom.

Ghost was there to close the door behind him.

They waited for the call to go out to the others. When none did, T-Rex opened the door again.

Their attention still on the helicopter, the four in the lobby talked quietly among themselves.

"There's the helicopter." A tall man with a solid black ski mask watched as the helicopter hovered over the parking lot. "Where the hell're the news people?" one of them said.

"At this point, I don't care," said a man in a camouflage ski mask. "I just want to be on that helicopter and on my way to the border."

"Shut up!" The black ski mask guy shook his rifle at his teammate. "We aren't going until we get our message across. This is a call to arms to the people of this country. Or did you forget?"

"I don't see anyone else joining our team," said the man with the camouflage ski mask. "It's too damned hot to be wearing all of this crap."

"It's been thirteen minutes and we still don't have a news crew." Black ski mask man jerked his head toward the camouflage man. "Bring one of the women out. We need to show them we mean business."

The camouflage man turned toward T-Rex and hurried past to the theater. The other three men in the lobby redirected their attention to what was happening in the parking lot.

"There's a news van pulling in now," another man said.

"They better be connected with the national news, or we're not dealing," black ski mask guy said.

"Going to the theater," T-Rex said softly into his mic.

"The gang is almost to the building. We'll follow," Ghost said.

T-Rex stepped out of the room and tiptoed after the camouflage masked man, praying he wouldn't start a chain reaction that would get all of the hostages killed.

"I DON'T KNOW how you did it." Brenda hugged Sierra. "I almost cried when they let the children go."

Clay had managed to convince their captors to release the children and two of the mothers, who escorted the kids out of the building. That left four women, one park ranger and the two politicians. They kept them separated on opposite sides of the theater. Clay was in charge of Sierra and the women, while a more volatile man had his weapon trained on the vice president, Ranger Jared and Grady Morris.

"Poor Stevie and Gemma." Sierra's heart squeezed

in her chest. "They didn't want to leave without their mothers."

"Yeah, but they're safe now."

"We hope." Sierra didn't know what had happened to them once the children left the theater. Clay had told them the children would be released unharmed.

In the meantime, she and the others were being held until the Free America group got what they wanted. What that was, Sierra didn't know.

After the children had been released, Clay stood for a moment talking to another member of the terrorist group. When that man left the theater, Clay walked down to where the women sat. He grabbed Sierra by the arm and yanked her to her feet, pulling her away from the other women. "I got your damned kids released, it's time you came with me." He dragged her toward the exit.

Sierra dug in her heals. "I'm not leaving until the others are released."

"You sure as hell are." His hold tightened on her arm. "You promised you'd come without argument if the brats were let loose." He shoved her up against the wall and pressed the rifle barrel against her throat.

Sierra didn't flinch, though the cool metal wedged against her neck made it difficult to breathe. "You heard me. Not until the others are released."

He sneered down at her, his face turning a mottle red. "So much for your word being good."

She snorted. "I learned from the best of liars."

He backhanded her so hard, her head snapped back and hit the wall. Sierra's ears rang and she saw stars, but she refused to pass out. "Besides, you can't just walk out of this now. This place has to surrounded by every law enforcement agency in the tristate area."

"I'll get you out. And we'll go far away from this hellhole."

She faced him, her jaw tight, her fists clenched by her side. "I'm not going with you."

For a long moment, Clay pressed the rifle barrel into her throat, his nostrils flaring. "Fine. You'll die with the rest of them." He shoved her toward the others so hard she fell to her knees.

Then he stood back and aimed his rifle at the four women, his eyes narrowed.

Sierra stood, squared her shoulders and joined the other women.

A moan came from the upper end of the theater.

Grady sat in a theater seat, rocking back and forth. "It wasn't supposed to happen like this," he muttered. "It wasn't supposed to happen like this."

"Shut up, Morris." The bad-tempered terrorist at the top of the theater hit Morris in the side of his head with the butt of his weapon.

Morris fell out of his seat onto the floor and curled into the fetal position, rocking and sobbing. "It wasn't supposed to happen this way."

"Hey." Bad-Tempered Guard got Clay's attention. "I gotta piss. When are we supposed to be replaced?"

"Hell if I know," Clay responded.

"I can't wait." Bad-Tempered Guard waved his rifle at the men. "Watch these three."

"Send someone else in," Clay said. "This is a lot of people for one guy to cover."

"So, you figured that out, did you? You didn't seem to think so when you left me alone a while ago." Bad-Tempered Guard snorted. "Seriously, shoot them if they look at you cross-eyed."

"Much as I'd like to do that, we can't," Clay said. "They're our tickets out of here. Without them, we're dead."

"We're dead anyway. You might as well take some of them with you." Bad-Tempered Guard left the theater.

Ellis moved to a more strategic position near their prize catch, the vice president. Then he alternated watching the three men at the top of the theater and the women down in front by the stage.

Sierra figured Clay couldn't keep a close eye on all of them all of the time, and she assumed the primary hostage was the vice president. He'd be more concerned about keeping the vice president from making an escape than a bunch of women.

"How long are you going to keep us here?" the vice president asked.

Clay turned his head to study the vice president and the congressional candidate. "As long as it takes to get what we came for."

Taking her chance while Clay's attention was diverted, Sierra inched toward the stage where Ranger Jared had set out a display of the various types of rock that could be found in Yellowstone National Park. She selected two particularly heavy and dense rocks the size of her palm and hid them behind her back. The stun gun would have been better, but it was in her purse halfway up the theater on the floor somewhere. She couldn't risk going after it now. Clay might figure out that was what she was getting from her purse, since she'd used it on him before.

She moved back in place before Clay shifted his attention back to her. She caught his glance and let her gaze drop first. Let him think he had her cowed and she wouldn't fight back. They needed all the advantages they could get. If they were going to make a move, it had to be before Bad-Tempered Guard returned. Sierra didn't want to test his commitment to killing all of them if anything went south on their operation.

The next time Clay glanced away, Sierra handed Brenda one of the rocks.

Clay looked back again, his eyes narrowing. He stared long and hard at Sierra.

"Kind of hard to keep an eye on two groups, don't you think?" she asked.

He glared at her. "I have it covered."

"Would it be easier if we moved up to the others?"

"I'll tell you what would be easier." His lip pulled back in an ugly snarl. "You keeping your mouth shut."

Sierra held up a hand. "Hey, I don't want to get shot any more than anyone else. If that means making it easier on you, so be it."

Clay chewed on her words for a moment and then nodded. "You four women, move up here."

Sierra hustled the women up to where the men sat at the top of the theater, grabbing another one of the big rocks from the display on the stage along the way, careful not to let Clay see what she was carrying by moving close to the other women.

Once they were with the men, Sierra slipped one of the rocks into Ranger Jared's hand. Then with the other one gripped firmly, she edged her way over to Clay. "I've been thinking."

Clay glared at her. "I don't care what you think. You lied to me."

"That's what I was thinking about. I guess I was

mad and wanted to get back at you for all the nasty, mean and horrible things you've done to me in the past."

"Where are you going with this? Because it's not convincing me I shouldn't shoot you."

"I don't want to die today. If it means leaving with you. I guess it's the only choice I have."

"Sorry, you had your chance. Now you're just one of the hostages." He jerked his head toward the others. "Get back with everyone else."

Sierra ignored his order and moved closer. If they wanted to get out of there, they had seconds to do it before Bad-Tempered Guard returned. "Clay, remember when we were kids and slipped beneath the bleachers to make out?"

"Where are you going with this, Sierra?" He pointed the barrel of the AR-15 rifle at her chest. "Get back with the others before I have to shoot you."

Sierra touched the tip of the barrel and pushed it gently to the side. "Don't you wish we could be that young and carefree again with our whole lives ahead and nothing to stop us?" She inched closer.

"There's no going back. You never loved me. I knew that the day we married."

She must have known it, too, but she shook her head. "We had it good for a while. We can do it again. If we try." Finally close enough to press her body against his, she wrapped one of her arms around his neck and leaned her breasts against his chest. Inside, she wanted to vomit. But on the outside, she hid her revulsion, thinking about the others in the room whose lives depended on her convincing Clay she still loved him and they had a chance at a life together. Which they didn't. No way in hell.

"Let's you and me get out of here. We'll start over." She kissed his chin and trailed her lips to his. "Let's leave now."

He crushed his mouth down on hers and dragged her body hard against his with his free hand.

Sierra raised her arm as if she would wrap it around his neck with the other. That was when she slammed the big rock to his temple, hitting him at the corner of his brow. Blood ran out of the gash into his eye.

Clay yelled and shoved her away, clamping a hand over the gash.

Before Clay could raise his weapon to fire, Sierra shoved the heel of her palm upward, catching Clay's nose, breaking it with a sickening crunch.

Since he was still standing and in the way of her freedom, Sierra kneed him in the groin. When he bent double, she slammed his head against her knee. "That's for all the times you hit me and I didn't know how to defend myself."

He fell to the floor. Out cold.

Sierra turned to the others. "Hurry! Let's get out

of here." She headed to the other door at the top of the theater. The one opposite from the one Bad-Tempered Guard had gone through, and hopefully farther away from the men in the lobby.

Sierra was first to the door. She pushed it open enough to see into the lobby. Men in ski masks were shouting. She couldn't tell if they were shouting at each other or someone else. Sierra didn't care.

She pointed to a potted plant in the hallway away from the theater. Turning to Brenda, she said, "Make it to the plant first. Watch them. When they aren't looking, head for the exit at the end of the hallway."

The men were so busy yelling at each other, they weren't watching the theater.

Sierra touched Brenda's shoulder. "Go. I'll send the others. Help them get out."

Brenda nodded and ran for the potted plant.

Her breath caught in her throat, Sierra held it until her friend made it to the plant and then the end of the hallway and out the door.

She pointed to the vice president. "You're next, sir."

He shook his head. "Ladies first. Get them safe." He urged one of the mothers forward.

She shrank back, shaking her head. "I can't."

"Then come with me." The other mother grabbed her hand and dragged her through the door and down the hallway.

Once the two mothers were gone, the vice president touched her shoulder. "You're next."

She stood fast. "I'm last out. Go, Mr. Vice President. You're the big fish they have to negotiate with. If they don't have you, they don't have their bargaining chip."

"I insist," the vice president said. "Please, don't hesitate. The sooner you're out, the sooner the rest of us will go."

Grady Morris erupted from the floor. "Out. I need out." He ran to the door and out into the hallway without looking first.

A shout sounded behind Sierra. Bad-Tempered Guard ran into the theater from the other door. "Damn it! What the hell's going on?"

"Go!" Sierra shoved Ranger Jared toward the door.

Jared ran down the hallway, not bothering to hide behind the potted plant.

The vice president refused to budge when Sierra tried to push him through the door. Instead, he stepped between her and Bad-Tempered Guard, blocking any bullets that might be aimed her way. "Go." He shoved her out the door and turned toward Bad-Tempered Guard. "Don't shoot!"

Sierra had two choices: run or be shot.

She ran.

Footsteps sounded behind her, and gunfire echoed off the high ceilings.

"Stop, or I'll shoot," a voice shouted.

Sierra wasn't stopping. She was halfway to the outside door. She couldn't slow her momentum, even if she'd wanted to.

Another shot was fired.

Pain blasted through her calf and sent her falling flat on her face. Her head hit the floor, rattling her brain, making her vision blur.

More shouts sounded in the lobby. Men scurried, more shots were fired.

Sierra pushed to her knees and tried to stand, but pain ripped up her leg and made her fall back to the ground.

An arm reached around her and pulled her off the floor and locked her against a tense body. Her captor spun with her, facing the melee, and shouted, "Try anything, and I'll kill her!"

Pain knifed through her leg, pushing fuzzy gray fog around her vision, but Sierra refused to pass out. Her vision cleared just enough to realize the men in ski masks lay littered across the lobby floor. Law enforcement personnel poured into the building, weapons drawn, ready to shoot anything that moved. In the middle of them stood a tall, dark, auburn-haired marine with wide hazel eyes.

T-Rex. And he looked scared.

Chapter Fifteen

T-Rex froze. A tall man in a dark ski mask held Sierra clamped to his side with one arm. In the opposite hand, he held a grenade.

"I've pulled the pin. If you shoot me, I'll release the handle. Sure, you'll kill me, but the woman dies, too."

T-Rex stepped forward, dropped his weapon to the ground and held up his hands. "Don't hurt her. She's done nothing to you."

"Yeah, well, she's going to get me out of here." The man waved the grenade. "If this goes off now, it will kill me, her and half of the people in this building. Do you want that?"

"No." Garner stepped up beside T-Rex. "No one will hurt you. What do you want?"

"I want that helicopter out there."

"You've got it." Garner turned to Caveman. "Get outside and clear a path to the chopper. Now!"

Caveman grabbed several deputies and ran out

the door. Through the windows, T-Rex could see them clearing all personnel out of the path between the visitors center and the helicopter.

"I'll need escorts to make sure no one takes a shot at me and the woman," the captor said. "Consider it more collateral to ensure I make it to the chopper without dropping this baby."

"You've got it," Garner said. "I'll escort you myself."

"Me, too," T-Rex added.

"Then let's get going before the woman bleeds out."

That was when T-Rex noticed the pool of blood on the floor beneath Sierra. His heart pinched hard in his chest. He stepped forward, wanting to go to her and apply pressure to the wound.

But the man with the grenade was calling the shots. One wrong move and the wound wouldn't matter anymore.

"Let's go!" Sierra's captor yelled. He shoved Sierra forward, holding her close, the hand with the grenade held high for all to see and fear.

T-Rex feared all right. He didn't see any way out of this scenario.

Sierra stared across at him, a crooked smile on her face. "I tried to escape. I guess I didn't do so good."

"We'll figure this out. Don't worry," T-Rex said.

"Shut up and keep moving," said the man with the grenade.

"Wait!" a shout went up. The vice president emerged from the theater, escorted by Ghost. "Leave the woman. Take me."

The captor snorted. "A little late for heroics. I want in that helicopter in the next two minutes, or I'll let go of this grenade. And I don't care if it kills every last one of you."

"Please, don't. We'll get you to the helicopter," Garner assured the man. "Step this way. No one will hurt you."

"Damn right, they won't. Not if they want her to live."

T-Rex moved to stand on the other side of Sierra and the man holding her hostage. Between him and Garner, they walked the pair to the exit, striding slowly to avoid any misinterpretation of their movements.

Garner was first through the door, holding up his hands as he went. "Don't shoot!"

The parking lot in front of them had been completely cleared of all personnel. Many of the vehicles had been moved to allow the helicopter to land on the pavement. There was a line of cars in the handicapped spots between the visitors center and the helicopter.

Once T-Rex stepped through and moved to the

side, the man with the grenade and Sierra emerged from the building. "Stay back at least ten yards," he said as he moved toward the parking lot and the helicopter.

T-Rex tried to think of a way to save Sierra. Perhaps if T-Rex threw himself at her captor and landed on the hand with the grenade, Sierra would be spared. He tried to calculate the amount of time it would take for him to close the distance between them and the number of seconds it would take before the grenade exploded. He couldn't risk it. If he didn't make it in time, the terrorist would drop the grenade and it would be the end of the terrorist, Sierra, T-Rex and Garner.

He'd never been faced with a scenario this important in his entire life. When Gunny had been hit, they hadn't known it was coming. They didn't have time to prepare.

Knowing what could happen was far worse. If that grenade dropped and he lived through the explosion, he'd forever wonder if Sierra would have survived if he'd chosen a different option.

He appeared to be faced with a no-win situation.

If the terrorist made it to the helicopter with Sierra, there was no telling what he'd do with her next.

T-Rex didn't want to think of the possibilities. He just wanted her safely away. Back in her room at the bed-and-breakfast, making love with him.

He wanted more time to get to know the brave woman and see if, as he suspected, they could be perfect for each other. He'd even consider giving up his military career to be with her. Anything. Just let her live.

SIERRA'S LEG HURT like hell, but she couldn't stand by and let this man get away with a government helicopter and possibly killing the pilot and copilot. As they neared the parked cars, she formed a plan in her head. It wasn't a good plan, but it was all she could think of. If she didn't do something quickly, T-Rex would try to save her, and then all hell would break loose.

T-Rex wouldn't let the terrorist leave the ground with Sierra. He'd do something horribly heroic like throw himself on the grenade. He was a good man with a lot of life ahead of him. He deserved to live it, not die taking one for the team or her.

Sierra couldn't let that happen.

In the time she had left, her mind flashed through what they had experienced together. It wasn't much, but their meeting and lovemaking had been intense and insanely satisfying. If only she had more time with him. If only she could have told him how she really felt about him.

If only she had another day to spend with T-Rex, she'd make the very most of it and savor it to the mo-

ment she died. All of this flashed through her mind
and filled her heart, swelling her chest. Mrs. McCall
had been right. In the couple of days she'd known
T-Rex, she'd fallen for the big marine.

Sierra could imagine spending the rest of her life
with such a man. Yeah, he'd be away a lot, and she'd
be worried when he was gone, but she'd love him
harder when he was with her. If only she'd had the
chance to convince him he deserved to be loved and
that he should give his lady love the choice of being
there when he came home from war.

The walk toward the helicopter was slow due
to her injured leg. She didn't have a chance of out-
running her captor. Whatever she did would require
her to sacrifice herself to make it happen. Because,
as the closest person to the man with the grenade, it
was up to her to do whatever it took to keep T-Rex,
Garner and the helicopter crew from bearing the
brunt of a terrorist's plan. Thankfully, her captor had
Garner and T-Rex back off to ten yards away from
where they were. It would help with her plan if they
had distance and cars between them.

As soon the terrorist marched her between two
cars on their way to the helicopter, Sierra turned to
T-Rex and dipped her head. Hoping he had caught
her meaning, Sierra made her move and pretended
to faint, letting her body go limp.

Her captor was thrown off balance and dipped

with her weight. In order to balance himself and catch her, he bent and lowered the arm carrying the grenade as her body sank toward the pavement.

Then when she thought the bulk of the explosion would be sandwiched between the cars, she bunched her legs and shot up fast and hard, hitting her head beneath the man's chin.

He loosened his hold on her and the grenade.

Sierra dropped to the ground and rolled beneath a car. The world around her exploded, rocking the vehicle above her so violently she knocked her head into the undercarriage.

Blackness claimed her.

T-REX HAD BEEN watching Sierra's face, worried she would bleed out before she even made it to the helicopter. Forced to maintain their distance, he was at a point with two vehicles between him and Sierra. He couldn't get to her fast enough to help her. He'd have to wait until they cleared the parked cars. But when her gaze darted to his and held, then she'd dipped her head, he knew she was going to try something.

He opened his mouth to shout *Don't do it.* But it was too late.

Sierra dropped toward the ground, as if she'd fainted.

"Get down!" T-Rex shouted as he ducked behind a vehicle. An explosion knocked him off his feet. A back flash filled his head of the Afghan village and the explosion that had crippled Gunny.

After the earth stopped shaking and the debris stopped falling, T-Rex rose from his position.

"Sierra?" he called out. "Oh, God, Sierra!" T-Rex ran around the front of the vehicle he'd ducked behind and nearly tripped over the hood of the next vehicle. It had been blown completely off the car. The top of the vehicle was mangled metal, and somewhere gasoline was leaking.

"Sierra!" T-Rex's stomach clenched as he looked between two horribly distorted vehicles to what was left of the terrorist. He held his breath, afraid of what he would find of Sierra.

She wasn't there.

T-Rex straightened and turned around. Had she been thrown clear of the vehicles? He didn't see her body lying anywhere close. "Sierra!"

A low moan sounded from beneath one of the cars.

T-Rex dropped down to his knees among the jagged metal and broken glass and peered beneath the chassis of what might once have been a sedan. A torn sleeve lay within inches of fingers. He reached for the fabric and nearly fell backward when it moved. A slim, feminine hand, marred with scratches and abrasions, reached toward him.

"Sierra?" He wrapped his fingers around hers

and held on. "Oh, baby, we'll get you out of there. Hold on."

Garner arrived first, then Caveman, Ghost and Hawkeye. With the help of the other law enforcement teams, they lifted what was left of the mangled car off Sierra.

The emergency medical team that had been on standby moved in and pulled her out.

By then, she wasn't moving. Her hand had gone limp in his as they lifted the heavy vehicle.

T-Rex followed the EMTs as they loaded her onto a backboard. "Is she…"

"Alive?" One medical technician glanced up. "Yes. But we need to get her to the hospital ASAP and check her for internal bleeding. We don't know what damage she might have sustained due to the explosion or being crushed by the car."

T-Rex bent to kiss her forehead and whispered, "I'll be there when you wake."

Then she was loaded into a medical helicopter and transported to the hospital in Bozeman, Montana.

T-Rex watched until the helicopter disappeared, his heart leaving with it. "I have to get to the hospital."

"We'll have the Army National Guard helicopter take you in a few minutes," Garner said. "I want to go with you, but I also want to get an assessment of the situation here before I leave."

"I don't give a damn about what's here. I need to be there when Sierra wakes."

Garner clapped a hand to T-Rex's back. "And I promise, you'll be there, as soon as I get a status."

The team gathered around the terrorist who'd taken Sierra captive.

"Grady Morris is back in the building, spilling his guts, hoping for a plea bargain for information," Ghost said. "He's pointing his finger at this guy as the ringleader."

"Who is this guy?" T-Rex asked, reaching down to pull the ski mask off what was left of the man who'd almost killed Sierra.

Even before T-Rex removed the mask from the man's head, Garner spoke, "What do you want to bet it's Fratiani?"

T-Rex removed the mask. The man lying in pieces was Leo Fratiani, the land broker who'd tried to purchase Olivia Dawson's ranch after her father was murdered.

T-Rex shook his head. "Why?"

"He thought he could get away with it," Ghost said. "Morris says Fratiani was an engineer on one of the pipeline projects and was laid off when the work dried up. Since then, he's lost his wife to divorce and his home to foreclosure. He tried his hand as a land broker in California, but when he tried to acquire his own properties, no bank would give him a loan. His credit was crap."

"Then how did he get the money to outfit the Free America group with AR-15s?" T-Rex asked.

"Grady Morris," Ghost responded.

"The politician?" Caveman shook his head. "Why the hell would Morris get involved with someone as shady as Fratiani?"

Ghost answered, "He wanted to stir things up in Wyoming so that he could appear to be the man people should vote for to clean up what was going on, and put people back to work on the pipeline."

"Bastard," T-Rex bit out.

Garner glanced at Ghost. "How's the vice president?"

"Unscathed," Caveman said.

"The other hostages?" T-Rex asked.

"No injuries to the hostages, other than Ms. Daniels." Ghost chuckled and smiled at T-Rex. "Apparently, your girlfriend got them out before the shooting began."

Sheriff Scott joined the Safe Haven team and faced Garner. "I want to thank you and your team for helping us diffuse the situation. None of our people were injured in the process. Of the Free America group, we have seven dead, three injured and eight who gave up when the shooting started."

T-Rex turned to Garner. "Everyone is accounted for. Can we go to the hospital now?"

Garner faced the sheriff.

"We'll take care of everything here." Sheriff Scott nodded toward the waiting helicopter. "Go."

T-Rex met Garner's gaze.

Garner turned to Ghost.

"We can catch a ride back to Grizzly Pass with some of the sheriff's people," Ghost said. "I'd like to stay and help with the cleanup."

The Homeland Security agent nodded to T-Rex. "Let's go."

They jogged to the waiting helicopter. Within minutes they were in the air and heading to the hospital. Eventually, they were touching down near the hospital in Bozeman. The pilots of the Black Hawk had to return to their post, leaving Garner and T-Rex to find their own way back.

T-Rex didn't care. His number one priority was to be at Sierra's side when she woke. She'd taken the fall to keep anyone else from being hurt by Fratiani. The woman had guts and a heart as big as the skies in Montana. She was more than he could have ever wanted in a woman, and, by God, he would be there when she opened her eyes. She didn't have anyone else. And he needed to be the first face she saw.

It didn't make any sense. All the years he'd refused to give his heart to a woman, knowing it wouldn't be fair to ask her to stick around while he was off fighting wars. But for once in his life, he wanted someone to be there when he came home. He wanted that someone to be Sierra. Call him selfish, but he wanted that more than he'd ever wanted anything.

Sierra was strong, determined and had a big, loving heart. She deserved to be happy. T-Rex wanted to be the man who made her happy. If he had to give up his career in the Marine Corps, he would.

He was led to the emergency room waiting area, where he paced for the next thirty minutes while they evaluated and worked on Sierra. When the ER doctor finally came out, he glanced around the waiting room. "Family of Ms. Daniels?"

T-Rex raised his hand and hurried forward.

"Are you her husband?"

He didn't hesitate. "Yes."

"The bullet went clean through her calf. There was some tissue damage, but we expect she will heal completely. She's also got a concussion. Considering she was in the path of a grenade explosion, we'd like to keep her overnight for observation. Other than that, she should be able to go home tomorrow."

T-Rex released the breath he'd been holding. "When can I see her?"

"Now. She's been moved to a room on the third floor."

"Is she conscious?"

He smiled. "Yes, and she's been asking for a dinosaur. Maybe you'll understand. Not just any dinosaur. She wants a—"

"T-Rex?" T-Rex's face split into a grin. "I know what she wants." He shook the doctor's hand. "Thank you." And he ran for the elevator.

He found her room and knocked on the door.

"Come in," a feminine voice called out.

T-Rex pushed open the door and walked in.

A nurse stood beside the bed, adjusted the IV and turned toward T-Rex. "You wouldn't happen to be T-Rex?"

He nodded. "Guilty."

She stepped back so that T-Rex could see Sierra lying against the sterile white sheets. "This the guy you've been looking for?"

Sierra's face and hands were covered in cuts and bruises, but her smile shined, lighting the room. "You came."

"Wild horses couldn't keep me away." He crossed to the bed and lifted her hand to his lips. "Hey, beautiful."

Her cheeks turned a pretty shade of pink. "I'm a mess. And my ears are ringing."

"You're alive, that's all that matters."

Her smile slipped and she studied him, sweeping her gaze over him from head to foot. "You and Garner?"

He chuckled. "Alive and well."

Her shoulders slumped. "Thank God. I worried my attempt to escape would get others hurt."

"On the contrary. Your attempted escape saved lives."

"And your team?"

"All made it unscathed. It appears you are the only casualty."

"Figures." Her pout made T-Rex want to kiss her even more.

Still holding her hand, he sat in the chair beside her bed. "You know, I've been rethinking the whole military career thing."

She frowned. "Oh yeah? I thought you had it all figured out."

"That was BS."

Sierra's frown deepened. "BS?"

He grinned. "Before Sierra."

"Oh." She blushed and glanced down at her hands. "And now?"

"I'm thinking Wyoming might be a good place to live. As a civilian."

Sierra shook her head. "Are you out of your mind? You're a career marine. Why would you want to give that up?"

He brought her hand to his lips and pressed a kiss to her knuckles. "I believe there just might be more to life than killing the enemy."

She squeezed his hand. "But the country needs you."

"I'm finding that I need you, and I want to be a little selfish for once in my lonely, miserable life."

Sierra's fingers tightened in his, and tears welled in her eyes. "But you don't like commitment."

He lifted his chin. "It's a guy's prerogative to change his mind." Then he winked. "What do you think? If I could find a job in Grizzly Pass, would you consider going out with me?"

She shook her head.

T-Rex's gut clenched. He hadn't thought through what he was going to say to her, but when he'd asked her out, he hadn't expected no for an answer. "Why not?"

"I am not going to be the woman responsible for taking you away from the military duty you love." She pinched the bridge of her nose. "You do love being a member of the Marine Corps, don't you?"

He nodded. "Yes, but—"

"Then why give it up?" She stared into his eyes. "I don't have anything keeping me in Grizzly Pass. I've always wanted to see other places." She dipped her head. "Just not by myself."

"You'd follow me?"

She nodded. "If things work out between us, I'd follow you to the ends of the earth."

He lifted her hand to his lips. "What if I asked to stay on here for a few more weeks? You know, give us a chance to get to know each other."

She looked up through eyes swimming in tears. "I'd like that."

"If I can't extend my TDY with the Department of Homeland Security, I'll ask for leave."

"Then we have a date?"

"More than one, I hope."

"So the big, tough marine is opening his heart to possibilities?"

He nodded. "To you."

"What made you change your mind?"

"Babe, I've never met a woman who'd be willing to take a grenade for me. How can I not fall in love with you?"

She laughed out loud, winced and pressed a hand to her head. "Don't count on me taking too many grenades."

"Trust me, one was more than my heart could take." He leaned forward and kissed her lips. "Sierra Daniels, I think I'm falling for you. Is it possible to fall in love so quickly?"

"Captain Rex Trainor, I have it from a good source, it doesn't take long if you fall for the right person." She wrapped her hand around the back of his head and deepened the kiss.

This was where T-Rex wanted to be. With this woman, where she was. Whether in Grizzly Pass or at one of his duty stations. As long as she was there when he got home, he'd keep coming home.

Chapter Sixteen

"Gunny, I can't tell you how glad I am to hear you're going to get the feeling back in your hands." T-Rex stood at the railing of the wide wraparound porch at Stone Oak Ranch, staring out at the Beartooth Mountains and the bright yellow sun shining down on them. Life couldn't get better.

"You and me both. I'm working on the legs next. I want to be up and running by the time my son turns four and starts training for football." Sounds interrupted Gunny, and a moment later he said, "I have to go. My wife has a chore for me to do. You know the saying, *Happy Wife, Happy Life.* I'll touch bases with you later this week to see how the dates are going. Treat her like a princess and you'll win her heart."

T-Rex ended the call on the cordless phone.

"I'll take that." Liv Dawson held out her hand for the phone and handed him a bottle of beer. "Are you about ready for a steak?"

"You bet." He walked down the steps to the grill where Hawkeye was flipping steaks. "Need a hand?"

"No. I've got this. I've already been assigned grill duty for when I retire from active duty. Liv is hopeless in the kitchen."

Liv handed Hawkeye a beer in exchange for a kiss. "I'm going to starve while you're gone."

"Six months. I put in my paperwork last night online. I'll be out of the army in six months."

"Then the real work begins. Are you sure you don't want me to sell this place and we both retire to a condo on the beach in Florida?" Liv slipped her arm around Hawkeye and leaned into him.

"Darlin', I love ranching. It's where I want to be."

"Glad to hear it." She stood on her toes to press a kiss to his lips. "Because there's a lot of work to be done and not nearly enough people to do it."

"CJ Running Bear is working out great. He's turned out to be an excellent ranch hand."

T-Rex glanced over to the teen sitting on the porch next to Lolly McClain, Charlie's six-year-old daughter. The young man had taken on a lot of responsibility and was helping his mother and siblings get back on their feet after losing his stepfather. "He's a good kid with a great work ethic. What if he wants to go to college or join the military?"

"We won't hold him back," Liv said.

Hawkeye nodded. "He deserves to follow his own

dreams. But until then, he's agreed to help out on the ranch."

T-Rex went in search of Sierra. He'd last seen her helping Charlie McClain in the kitchen cutting up onions, lettuce and tomatoes for those who preferred hamburgers to steaks.

He found Charlie, but not Sierra. And Charlie was in Ghost's arms, kissing him.

T-Rex grinned. "You two need a room?"

Ghost broke the kiss and took a swing at T-Rex's shoulder. "We have a room, in a house we found online back at my duty station. Charlie and Lolly are moving in with me until I can make an honest woman out of her."

Charlie held up her hand, sporting a diamond ring on her left finger. "We're engaged," she said.

"That's wonderful!" Grace Saunders exclaimed and climbed the steps up to the porch to see the ring. "You three will make a great family."

T-Rex pounded Ghost on the back. The SEAL was obviously in love with Charlie. "And you're not staying in Grizzly Pass?"

Ghost shook his head. "I have a few more years before I can retire. Then we might consider return-ing to Wyoming."

"Until then, I can take my work anywhere there's internet." Charlie wrapped her arms around Ghost's middle. "Wherever Ghost goes, I'll follow."

Ghost kissed the tip of her nose. "Except when I deploy."

She laughed. "True. But Lolly and I will be waiting for you to come home."

T-Rex turned to Grace, the naturalist who studied the wolves of Yellowstone National Park. "What about you and Caveman? Are you leaving Wyoming to follow Caveman wherever the Delta Force takes him?"

Grace shook her head and smiled toward Caveman. "I can't give up my work. There's so much more to learn from the wolves we've reintroduced to the ecosystem here."

Caveman joined her and draped an arm over her shoulders. "I'm three months shy of my reenlistment. I've decided to leave the military. But I have a job waiting for me when I get back to Wyoming."

"He's coming to work for me," Kevin Garner called out from the horseshoe pit where he was playing against his wife, Kathleen.

Everyone seemed to have figured out where they were going. He couldn't be happier for the team he'd come to care about.

T-Rex looked around and finally spotted Sierra. She was coming toward him with a cookie in her hand. "Miss me?"

"You bet." He kissed her lips and then took a bite of the cookie. "You know, when I retire, I wouldn't mind coming back to Grizzly Pass. The place grows on you."

"I'm glad you think so." She leaned against him, fitting perfectly in the crook of his arm.

Together they stood at the porch railing, watching the sun set on the mountain.

T-Rex couldn't believe how lucky he was. He'd found the perfect mate in Sierra, and he didn't want what they had together to ever end.

Sierra was amazing. She'd taught him so much. T-Rex finally understood that love was something you had to grab when you could for as long as you could. No regrets.

* * * * *

Don't miss the previous books in the
BALLISTIC COWBOYS series:

HOT COMBAT
HOT TARGET
HOT ZONE

Available now from Harlequin Intrigue!

COMING NEXT MONTH FROM

◆ HARLEQUIN®

INTRIGUE

Available July 18, 2017

#1725 DARK HORSE
Whitehorse, Montana: The McGraw Kidnapping
by B.J. Daniels
The case of the infant McGraw twins' kidnapping has been a mystery for
twenty-five years, and true-crime writer Nikki St. James means to crack it wide
open—but the protective Cull McGraw is wary of her intentions toward his
family...and toward him.

#1726 CORNERED IN CONARD COUNTY
Conard County: The Next Generation • by Rachel Lee
With a killer hot on her heels, Dory Lake seeks refuge in Conard County and
protection from one of Cadell Marcus's expertly trained guard dogs—but she
didn't count on Cadell as part of the deal.

#1727 PROTECTION DETAIL
The Precinct: Bachelors in Blue • by Julie Miller
Jane Boyle's life depends on her ability to keep secrets, and detective
Thomas Watson doesn't realize the nurse caring for his ailing father is in witness
protection...or that the sparks flying between them put them both at risk.

#1728 MANHUNT ON MYSTIC MESA
The Ranger Brigade: Family Secrets • by Cindi Myers
Ranger Ryan Spencer always follows the rules...until a murder investigation
leads him to bending a few for the sake of Jana Lassiter, and breaking them
completely when she's captured by the killer.

#1729 SECRET AGENT SURRENDER
The Lawmen: Bullets and Brawn • by Elizabeth Heiter
DEA agent Marcos Costa is undercover and ready to bring down a drug
kingpin inside his own mansion—until he runs into Brenna Hartwell, his very
first love. He doesn't know she's a rookie detective on a case, and their sweet
reunion will be short-lived if their cover is blown.

#1730 STONE COLD UNDERCOVER AGENT
by Nicole Helm
Undercover FBI agent Jaime Alessandro has seen nothing but darkness as
he's climbed the ranks of a crime ring. But when "The Stallion" makes him a
gift of Gabriella Torres, who has been a captive for eight years, he sees her as
much more than the key to bringing down the ring once and for all...

**YOU CAN FIND MORE INFORMATION ON UPCOMING HARLEQUIN® TITLES,
FREE EXCERPTS AND MORE AT WWW.HARLEQUIN.COM.**

HICNM0717

"I want to ask you about your babies," Nikki said. "Oakley and
Jesse Rose?" Was it her imagination or did the woman clutch
the dolls even harder to her thin chest?

"What happened the night they disappeared?" Did Nikki
really expect an answer? She could hope, couldn't she? Mostly,
she needed to hear the sound of her voice in this claustrophobic
room. The rocking had a hypnotic effect, like being pulled
down a rabbit hole.

"Everyone outside this room believes you had something to
do with it. You and Nate Corwin." No response, no reaction to
the name. "Was he your lover?"

She moved closer, catching the decaying scent that rose from
the rocking chair as if the woman was already dead. "I don't
believe it's true. But I think you might know who kidnapped
your babies," she whispered.

The speculation at the time was that the kidnapping had been
an inside job. Marianne had been suffering from postpartum
depression. The nanny had said that Mrs. McGraw was having
trouble bonding with the babies and that she'd been afraid to
leave Marianne alone with them.

And, of course, there'd been Marianne's secret lover—the man everyone believed had helped her kidnap her own children. He'd been implicated because of a shovel found in the stables with his bloody fingerprints on it—along with fresh soil—even though no fresh graves had been found.

"Was Nate Corwin involved, Marianne?" The court had decided that Marianne McGraw couldn't have acted alone. To get both babies out the second-story window, she would have needed an accomplice.

"Did my father help you?"

There was no sign that the woman even heard her, let alone recognized her alleged lover's name. And if the woman had answered, Nikki knew she would have jumped out of her skin.

She checked to make sure Tess wasn't watching as she snapped a photo of the woman in the rocker. The flash lit the room for an instant and made a snap sound. As she started to take another, she thought she heard a low growling sound coming from the rocker.

She hurriedly took another photo, though hesitantly, as the growling sound seemed to grow louder. Her eye on the viewfinder, she was still focused on the woman in the rocker when Marianne McGraw seemed to rock forward as if lurching from her chair.

A shriek escaped her before she could pull down the camera. She had closed her eyes and thrown herself back, slamming into the wall. Pain raced up one shoulder. She stifled a scream as she waited for the feel of the woman's clawlike fingers on her throat.

But Marianne McGraw hadn't moved. It had only been a trick of the light. And yet, Nikki noticed something different about the woman.

Marianne was smiling.

Don't miss
DARK HORSE by B.J. Daniels,
available August 2017 wherever
Harlequin® Intrigue books and ebooks are sold.

www.Harlequin.com

HIEXP0717

Reward the book lover in you!

Earn points from all your Harlequin book purchases from wherever you shop.

Turn your points into *FREE BOOKS* of your choice
OR
EXCLUSIVE GIFTS from your favorite authors or series.

Join for FREE today at
www.HarlequinMyRewards.com.

Harlequin My Rewards is a free program (no fees) without any commitments or obligations.

MYR17

Need an adrenaline rush from nail-biting tales
(and irresistible males)?

Check out **Harlequin® Intrigue®**
and **Harlequin® Romantic Suspense** books!

New books available every month!

CONNECT WITH US AT:

Harlequin.com/Community

ReaderService.com

**ROMANCE WHEN
YOU NEED IT**

SGENRE2017